Out of her element . . .

The dinghy taunted Koby. If she jumped in *Titmouse*, she could bring help in twenty minutes. All she had to do was let go of the big dorsal fin in her hand. But she still felt Lady's faint heartbeat. It held her like handcuffs, spellbound and helpless.

"I guess we're all stranded," Koby said aloud. The thought made her shiver.

Now dusk left only a pale red glow to stain the horizon. Lights blinked on along the shore. A string of cars threaded their way across Three-Mile Bridge, looking like a parade of tiny fireflies. Two more boats passed by, miles away. Koby knew that staying any longer was foolish, but she could not let go. Squirt stared helplessly. Lady's faint heartbeat tickled like a weak and distant drum. To leave would be to let Lady and Squirt die. The ebbing water splashed lower, tugging.

As darkness settled in, Koby made up her mind. "I'm staying!" she announced. "No matter what!"

BEN MIKAELSEN

STRANDED

Hyperion Paperbacks for Children
New York

This book is dedicated to
Trish and Alex,
two short-finned pilot whales
found stranded off Key West, Florida.

———————

On August 11, 1991,
after many weeks of volunteered care,
Trish and Alex were released back to their home,
the Atlantic Ocean.

First Hyperion Paperback edition 1996.
Text ©1995 by Ben Mikaelsen.
A hardcover edition of *Stranded* is available from Hyperion Books for Children.

Printed in the United States of America.

5 7 9 10 8 6 4

The text for this book is set in 12-point Janson.

Library of Congress Cataloging-in-Publication Data
Mikaelsen, Ben
Stranded / Ben Mikaelsen—1st ed.
p.   cm.
Summary: Twelve-year-old Koby, who has lost a foot in an accident, sees
a chance to prove her self-reliance to her parents when she tries to rescue
two stranded pilot whales near her home in the Florida Keys.
ISBN 0-7868-0072-0 (trade)—0-7868-2059-4 (lib. bdg.)—0-7868-1109-9 (pbk.)
[1. Whales—Fiction. 2. Wildlife rescue—Fiction. 3. Physically handi-
capped—Fiction 4. Florida Keys (Fla.)—Fiction. 5. Self-reliance—Fiction.]
I. Title.
PZ7.M5926St   1995
[Fic]—dc20   94-27069

I would like to acknowledge the generous assistance
provided by the owners and staff of Dolphins Plus
in Key Largo, Florida.
I would also like to acknowledge the help of the sailors,
scientists, marine biologists, veterinarians, fishermen,
family counselors, reporters, orthotists,
real-life Pod Squad members,
and all the others who made this book possible.
A special thanks to my editor, Andrea Cascardi,
for her patience and insights.
Also thanks to Karrie and Melissa
for allowing me inside your worlds.

ONE

Koby Easton remembered her first life. It had ended four years ago with the accident when she was eight. Only one thing could help her to forget that day.

The ocean.

She flexed her wrist to rev the ten-horse outboard and circled toward home. Her dinghy surged forward, bucking against the choppy waves. Sheets of spray lashed at the bow. It was late, and her faded one-piece swimsuit did little to ward off the chill edging the breeze. In the bow a cobia curled around in a circle. The big fish had fought for nearly a half hour before tiring.

Ahead, the sun hovered above the horizon like a glowing balloon. By now Mom would be worrying herself into a knot, Koby thought, aiming the dinghy toward the east end of Lonesome Key. She called the small inflatable boat *Titmouse* because it made her feel like one. A tufted titmouse was a happy-go-lucky, scruffy little bird that played on the ends of twigs, hanging upside down. That's what the dinghy did—it helped Koby swing upside down in life. Holding the bowline with her free hand, she grinned. The salty spray stung at her lips and cheeks as she tilted her head back. Her long brown hair whipped itself into tangled strands.

Out here there were no problems, no rules, no homework, no parents arguing. Out here Koby could even forget the accident. She looked down at the space below her right knee. Her right foot should have filled that hollow void. But it didn't.

She could still feel the phantom foot, still bend the missing ankle, still feel it cramp, still feel an itch between the toes. But only in her mind. Her leg ended in a fleshy stump halfway down her shin.

Her artificial foot bounced about in the netted pocket beside the seat. She called it her leggy—she would never call it her leg. Onshore she might need two feet, but in this flat watery world Koby didn't have to wear the chipped and phony-looking chunk of plastic. Out here there was nobody to stare. Nobody to whisper. Out here she could try and forget that day when a speeding car had wrecked her bicycle—and her life.

Koby squinted into the wind. Ahead, the Florida Keys rimmed the horizon. Southward, the ocean stretched forever until it bumped into a faded blue sky. Nothing in all the world seemed so desolate and empty. That was only how it looked, Koby mused. That was only the top. A strange and eerie world lurked below the surface. She let her gaze sweep the horizon. The ocean was so big she could see the curving of the earth. Someday she wanted to go over that curve and beyond and never come back. Someday.

With her head turned, Koby did not see a dark shape roll in

the swell directly ahead—not until it was nearly too late. She swerved sharply and braced for impact. The dinghy veered out of control and pitched to a stop. Nothing hit. A stern wave rolled up from behind, rocking *Titmouse* dangerously. Koby lost her balance and fell onto the slimy cobia. A wave washed over the side. The motor stalled.

With water sloshing about, Koby scrambled to her knees and peered over the bow. Bright reflections glazed the surface. Was she imagining things?

"No!" she whispered—something black had broken the surface. Squinting, she searched. Long seconds passed, then minutes. Finally she turned back to restart the outboard. That's when it happened.

Air exploded! Beside the dinghy, a fin broke the surface.

Koby spun around. "Shark!" she gasped. The fin rose higher, exposing a torpedolike body that stretched nearly twice the length of the ten-foot dinghy. Koby stared in disbelief—it *wasn't* a shark. Nor was it a dolphin.

It was a small whale drifting ghostlike in the rough water only yards away. A molded smile creased its face. Ragged and wheezing breaths belched from the blowhole on its head. Koby wrinkled her nose and turned away from the rotten smell.

When she looked back, she spotted tangled shrimp netting knotted around one flipper. Another section of net had snagged on the animal's broad tail fluke. Tight knots and deep raw cuts served as grisly proof of how long the whale had struggled. Wild, glassy fear glinted in its eyes—fear and something else.

Koby had seen the same haunted stare once in the eyes of a manatee. Hit by a boat, the gentle underwater sea cow had rocked helplessly against the shore before dying.

Koby dared not leave to get help. In rough open water, it would be hard to find the whale again.

"Don't give up," she said, looking about.

She had to do something, but what? Her gaze fell on the sheathed diving knife bouncing against her plastic leggy. Also in the side pocket were her dive mask and fin.

Quickly she grabbed the sharp knife. The strong ocean breeze and the tidal current were drifting her away from the whale. Using the oar, she paddled carefully back alongside the massive creature. If it thrashed its tail, *Titmouse* could capsize.

The whale's barrel-like body was swollen and puffy. Its tail looked like a smooth and worn mud flap off a big truck. Koby leaned out and grabbed a strand of nylon netting. Gently she pulled.

"Easy, fella. Easy," she whispered.

Again the whale puffed hard. The misty breath caught Koby in the face with a rotted musky smell. She cut at the netting with the knife. Instead of struggling, the whale hung still, listing sideways. It appeared dead except for the fear-glazed stare and sporadic breathing. Every breath rasped.

A big wave rocked the dinghy. Koby slipped forward, grabbing for the bowline to keep from falling overboard. It was hard bracing herself with only one foot and her stump. She kept hacking at the web of nylon. Accidentally she nicked the whale's rubbery black skin. Blood oozed from the cut. There were many other scrapes and cuts. Some had grown over with white puffy skin. Some glistened red. The deepest cut circled the right flipper. There the netting had cinched so tightly that an inch-deep gash spread open. Leaking blood clouded the water.

Koby fingered the knife nervously. Ocean currents carried smells like the wind. Sharks a mile away could zero in on the faintest trace of blood. Healthy, a whale could kill a shark. Wounded like this, there would be little fight. Injuries sure wrecked lives, Koby thought bitterly.

She kept slashing at the stiff and tangled nylon. As it fell away she threw the loose strands into the dinghy. This nylon netting would *never* trap another animal.

Time stood still while she worked. Koby's arm muscles throbbed, and her stump ached from being bumped. As the last few strands broke free, Koby let the whale drift clear. His gaze had dulled.

"Swim, fella. Try to swim!" Koby coaxed.

The whale puffed and sucked a weak breath through its blowhole. Barely had the little valve of skin closed on its back when a wave broke, tilting the whale on its side. He flopped weakly and righted, blow-gasping another breath.

Koby raised a worried look at the sun sinking into the water. Mom would be having guppies. If Dad was home, Mom would be arguing with him, telling him if he cared for his daughter he would be out looking for her. Dad would be making Mom more angry by telling her to quit worrying like a mother hen.

Koby wished her parents wouldn't argue over her. She was in the seventh grade now and could run her own life. She used the oar to keep herself alongside the whale. Each frantic breath sounded loudly with high-pitched squeaks and whistles. Then the whale arched deliberately and let out a creaky hinge sound. Its gaze grew intense.

That's when Koby first glimpsed something attacking the whale's belly. It looked like a small shark. The water's reflections made everything shimmer and dance in distorted patterns. Koby worked to position herself so the setting sun did not blind her. If it was a shark, why did it just hang there? It should be twisting, ripping, and tearing—trying to kill. Maybe it knew its prey was dying.

The whale convulsed, trying to shake away the attacker. Suddenly a bloody cloud muddied the water. Koby scrambled forward. "Don't kill him!" she shouted, her voice quavering. Desperately she stabbed the oar into the water, trying to hit whatever was attacking. She missed. The clouded water made her afraid she might strike the whale. Shaking, she waited in the bow, the oar held ready above her shoulder like a spear.

TWO

Gradually the water cleared. Still gripping the oar, Koby took a sharp breath and blinked hard.

"A calf!" she exclaimed. "A calf—you had a baby!"

An umbilical cord joined the wounded whale and her newborn calf like a knotted telephone cord. The baby arched, stretching the creases on its shiny body. It hung in a dark diluted pool of birth fluids and blood.

The mother flopped her gashed flipper. Still the umbilical cord held like a leash. She rolled and twisted harder, snapping the cord near the baby's wrinkled body. The calf's tail flukes were curled and its dorsal fin lay sideways from being in the womb.

At first Koby smiled. Then her fascination turned to horror. The calf drifted downward. Awkwardly the mother nosed at the baby, but it slipped away from her. Koby's thoughts scrambled. Her friend at the dock, an old sea captain named Nickeljack, claimed that with dolphins, younger females often acted as midwives and helped a weakened mother push her baby to the surface for its first breath. But today there were no midwives.

The waves pummeled the big whale's body. Several yards away, the newborn calf continued to drift deeper. He appeared to flop. Again the exhausted mother nosed roughly at her young. The desperate movement shoved the calf even deeper. Finally the mother surfaced and let out a long defeated whistle.

"He needs air!" Koby shouted.

The calf disappeared. He was drowning. Like a person, he was drowning! Koby grabbed the anchor and heaved it overboard. Line paid out rapidly but slackened after a few seconds as the anchor bottomed. Quickly she slipped on her face mask and her single flipper. She hesitated as she licked salt spray from her lips. Healthy, the mother whale would kill anything that approached her baby. Wounded, she might still try.

Koby adjusted her mask and plunged overboard. Cool salt water swirled and bubbled around her. She surfaced to breathe, then dived, twisting, kicking, searching.

At first nothing. Then, thirty feet away, she spotted a dim form drifting downward. Koby needed more air. Again she surfaced, breathed hard, and dived. She pinched her nose and blew to equalize the pressure on her ears. Even as Koby swam downward, the calf sank deeper.

The telltale ache for air gnawed at Koby's lungs. Mouth closed, she tried to yawn at the building pressure in her ears. She kicked harder. Stroke after stroke, she drew closer. With a last jerky lunge she reached the motionless calf and grabbed it by its soft flippers. The calf, nearly as big as she, slipped awkwardly from her grip. She fumbled and tried to shove it upward.

Again the smooth skin slipped through her grasp like a slick inner tube.

Normally Koby breathed deeply for several minutes before a dive. Not having done so made her lungs feel on fire. She hugged the calf tightly to her body. The warmth of its slippery body surprised her. She kicked upward. Bright shafts of brackish sunlight filtered down through the waves—the surface had to be near. Koby blinked hard. All her feelings were melting together and burning up her insides. She clenched her teeth, wanting to scream. If she let go of the calf, she could surface in seconds. She hugged harder and kicked furiously.

With the calf's head pressed against her cheek, she felt the faint but rapid pulsing of a heartbeat. It excited her. Now the surface hovered overhead like a transparent shimmering sheet. Air! Within arm's reach!

As her chest threatened to explode, Koby broke the surface. She gulped and gasped for air. Releasing the calf, she shoved her mask up and coughed.

The baby whale awoke as if from sleep. It thrashed its stiff tail and sculled at the water. A loud popping sounded through its blowhole. Nearby, the mother floated motionless. She seemed unaware of anything. Koby noticed the current had drifted them a stone's throw away from the anchored dinghy. An easy swim, she thought. On the horizon, the last glimmer of the setting sun had blinked from sight.

After more popping breaths, the calf flopped hard and disappeared, then surfaced with a clumsy leap. Misty breaths puffed from its blowhole as it circled.

"Over there!" Koby shouted, pointing toward the mother.

The calf moved the wrong way, making shrill squeaks.

"Over there!" Koby screamed.

It was no use—the calf splashed outward and away. Koby started swimming after it, then stopped and instead headed cautiously toward the mother. Any moment the big whale might come alive and attack.

"Easy, big lady. Call your baby," Koby cooed, swimming alongside.

The whale stared vacantly.

"Call your baby!" Koby said louder. She reached out and touched the rubbery dark skin. The movement seemed to startle the floating giant. Alertness glimmered in her eyes, and she let out a long scratchy moan. Koby tensed.

In the distance the calf turned at the sound. He splashed his tail and squirted under the waves. Almost instantly he surfaced alongside the mother, blowing hard.

"You did it, Lady!" Koby exclaimed. "You called your baby!"

She pulled her mask back over her eyes and submerged to look at the calf. Vertical creases, from being crowded inside the mother, circled the small body. His fluke and fin remained curled. Deliberately, the calf nuzzled and nudged along the mother. He stopped at a narrow slit under her tail and bunted at the opening. Tiny bubbles rose. Small puffs of milk clouded the water.

THREE

Koby watched the calf nurse until it broke free to blow for air. Traces of white milk trailed out from the mother's nursing slit. She could have been asleep except for her hollow stare—like big cow eyes.

Koby kicked forward smoothly. "Easy, Lady. Easy," she whispered, placing a hand under the mother's chin. Petting the skin was like rubbing a slippery watermelon. Slowly Koby brought her hand up and stroked the whale's face. Except for cuts, the skin felt firm and glassy. The mother's eyes turned downward as her calf slipped under the surface to nurse again.

A wave rolled in hard from the side. Koby came up coughing and spitting salt water. Catching her breath, she rubbed her hand under the whale's big barrel chest. The deeply gashed flipper twitched. Then Lady arched to clear her blowhole. The calf stopped nursing and flopped to the surface with a coltish spasm. A splash doused Koby and the mother.

"Careful!" Koby warned. "Don't hit Lady—that's your mom." She glanced nervously westward. Only a hint of yellow daylight still stained the horizon. Disturbingly far away, *Titmouse* bobbed at anchor. Soon the ocean would become inky black. Koby forced her hand away from Lady's body.

"I'm drifting too far from *Titmouse*," she said. "I have to go." She tried to talk softly, but her voice trembled.

Lady's gaze flickered.

Koby kept treading water, held there by something silly. She had called the mother Lady, but the baby still didn't have a name. All her animal friends had names: Frank, the big green moray eel that ate from her hand out on Chissom Reef; Charlie, the white heron at the harbor dock. Neither Frank nor Charlie approached anyone but her. It made her feel special.

With a swish of his tail, the calf darted under the mother.

"Squirt!" Koby exclaimed. "You're a Squirt!" The calf responded with a clumsy belly flop. Satisfied, Koby turned and wearily began the long swim back to the dinghy.

As she swam, the ebbing tide pushed against her like an invisible hand. She kicked and stroked harder. Even when her arms ached, she did not pause. She stroked and breathed, stroked and breathed, allowing only brief glances up to keep her course. It was possible for a tidal current to wash somebody out to sea.

When Koby finally grabbed the lifeline that circled the dinghy, she clung to the side, shaking and weak. She glanced back. No longer were the whales visible in the gathering darkness. Lazy waves slapped at *Titmouse*'s bow. Far away a single star twinkled above a sliver of moon.

With a hard kick, Koby dragged herself aboard and splashed onto the floor. She lay there trembling. By now Mom would be pacing up and down the deck of their home, a fifty-foot Gulf-star sailboat named *Dream Chaser*. She'd be gazing beyond the breakwater for any sign of *Titmouse*. Dad probably wasn't even home yet.

Koby noticed a dimmer star had joined the first one. Still breathing hard, she stowed her fin and mask and hauled up the anchor. Tonight the anchor weighed a ton. Next she gripped the engine's starter rope and tugged.

The engine seemed to sense her weariness and started obediently. *Titmouse* wallowed forward. Water sloshed about in the bottom. Koby fumbled to pull the plug out of the transom. Dad had taught her this trick. Under way, water drained out and not in—this saved bailing. As the bottom emptied, the dinghy gathered speed, chattering across the inky black surface. Soon Koby replaced the plug.

Along the approaching shoreline, the lights from Lonesome Key flickered in a long string. Lonesome Key stretched ten miles long, one of many such small islands stringing between Miami and Key West, Florida. The necklace of land separated the Atlantic Ocean from the Gulf of Mexico.

Koby debated her course home. *Dream Chaser* floated at anchor in Pelican Harbor on gulfside. From here there were three ways back.

Around the north end would be the safest but the farthest. South under Three-Mile Bridge would take her across the shallow sand flats. Idling through the flats at night took forever and was dangerous. Koby squinted at her third choice—a dark gap in the shore lights. That was Colter's Cut, a twisting channel of water that wound through a maze of mangrove trees. It crossed the middle of Lonesome Key over to gulfside.

Most people didn't go through Colter's Cut at night. There were stories of people who had and were never found again. Some said that killer alligators from the Everglades ate them. Some figured they got lost and floated around until the seagulls picked the meat off their bones.

Koby smiled. She loved the stories. She loved the creepy feeling that inched up her spine. Even when she was younger she enjoyed exploring dark places. Other kids cringed and held their breath watching her tiptoe up into a dark attic. Colter's Cut at night was the ultimate dark attic. The very thought filled Koby with shivering excitement. She breathed out slowly as she aimed the bow straight for shore. Tonight she pretended the dark ominous space was a monster's mouth.

In minutes she neared the inlet and throttled back. The shallow water and the thick groves of trees blended with the black sky. Several hours from now the stingy moon would be higher, dimly lighting the twisted passage. Then it would be no fun. Koby motored ahead, gripping the throttle so hard her knuckles hurt.

Even Dad didn't like coming here at night. He didn't mind if she did, though. He told her that, having lost a foot, she needed to try things on her own. Mom was just the opposite. She acted as if even a shadow were dangerous.

Protected by the mangroves, the water flattened into a slick calm. A cut like this was where Dad said they would bring the sailboat if ever they needed to ride out a hurricane. Koby squinted, prying at the darkness. The shrill screech of a night heron pierced the engine's hum. The laughing cry of a tern echoed back. Koby shivered. Ahead, dim waterways branched off, forming a deadly maze. No longer was there a shoreline. Tangled roots rose out of the water like bent arms waiting to grab the dinghy. Lights from town cast an eerie glow above the mangrove trees.

Suddenly the dinghy rammed a bank of roots. Koby sprawled forward, striking her stump on the oar. "Ouch!" she grunted, rubbing the tender bulb of skin. Luckily the roots had not punctured the dinghy. She backed away and continued more cautiously.

Twenty minutes later, Koby motored around the last bend into open water. Her eyes stung from squinting so hard. She stopped and pulled her damp sock from the side pocket of the dinghy. Carefully she stretched this and a padded insert over her stump. Next she pulled on her leggy. She tightened the strap above her knee with a final tug to keep the plastic foot from popping off.

Downshore the lights of Pelican Harbor sparkled out over the water. Koby gunned the engine. In minutes she banked into the protected inlet. Their home rested at anchor about two hundred yards out from the dock.

Deliberately Koby slowed and idled among the small community of live-aboard boats. Although storms rocked these boats half upside down, neighbors blew a cork if somebody's wake caused milk to spill. The motor sputtered to a stop as *Titmouse* drifted alongside *Dream Chaser*.

Koby's mom, Paige Easton, stood waiting on the deck of the long and shiny sailboat. Koby could recognize her long hair, baggy shorts, and tanned thin figure anywhere. Everybody thought Mom was pretty.

"Where have you been, honey?" Paige called. "I've been worried sick."

"Mom, a whale was hurt. She had a baby, and I saved it!"

"You what?" Paige's voice showed disbelief.

"Out near Chissom Reef, I found a whale in a net." Quickly Koby explained all that had happened.

Paige reached and tied off the bowline. "Do you know what time it is?"

Koby held up chunks of the tangled shrimp net. "I couldn't just leave the whales. If you want, I'll take you out and show them to you."

"Not at night, young lady. How was I to know you weren't hurt or drowning somewhere?"

"Mom, you always think something bad will happen."

Paige answered by glancing down at Koby's leggy.

FOUR

Koby glanced ashore. Dad's lobster boat, the *Lazy Mae*, was already tied up in its slip near the boathouse. "Where's Dad?" she asked.

"Who knows? He sure isn't counting his money!" Paige pointed. "Get that fish cleaned, then come below. You have school in the morning." She grabbed the handrails and swung easily down the companionway into the main salon.

Koby lifted the heavy cobia aboard and hauled it back to the stern for cleaning. With practiced hands, she chopped off the head and slit the belly open. She cut fast, trimming the meat from the bones. When she finished, she saved the head and guts to bait crab pots. The fish steaks she wrapped and took below to the freezer.

"Hurry and clean up," Paige said. "I'll reheat your supper."

Obediently Koby headed to her room, the small V-shaped cabin in the bow. With a sharp tug, she pulled off her leggy. After hanging her padded insert up to dry, she climbed into the cramped shower. If the salt water wasn't washed from her stump, the fleshy bulb of skin became raw and sore.

As she finished, she heard Dad's dinghy motoring out from shore. Quickly she slipped into a nightshirt. Without her leggy, she hopped past the galley and bounced her way topside. She got around the boat just fine on one leg.

Dutch Easton motored into the dim glow of the cabin lights. His curly white beard and big shoulders made him look like a pirate. He sat in his dinghy as relaxed as if resting on a couch.

Dutch flashed a careless smile as he threw Koby his bowline. "I missed you on the *Lazy Mae*—did you go fishing?" Grabbing the rail, he swung aboard.

"I got a big cobia." Proudly Koby opened the cooler and pointed at the head. "You know what else?" Excitedly she told about the whales. "And there's the netting I cut off," she said, pointing at *Titmouse*.

With gear under one arm, Dutch hugged her shoulders. "You're quite the one-legged pirate."

Koby didn't like when Dad treated her like a kindergartner. "You believe me, don't you?" she said.

Dutch acted shocked. "Of course I do. I believe anything my little mate says." He looked down and winked.

"Dad, I'm telling the truth. They're inside Chissom Reef somewhere."

"Okay, you show me in the morning."

"I would if you'd go out with me like you always promise."

Dutch scowled. "Sometimes I'm busy, mate. I said we'll run out in the morning, and we will!"

Koby nodded weakly.

Dutch whistled to her. "Here, take these bugs below and see

if Mom will cook up a snack." He threw over a burlap bag with lobster.

"Mom's already fixing food," Koby whispered.

Dutch motioned. "Go on, I'll be right down."

Koby opened the bag and counted five lobsters. Dad always called them bugs because with their beady eyes and antennae they looked like gigantic beetles. "Here, Mom," she said, climbing down the companionway. She dumped the lobsters into the galley sink. "Dad brought these for supper."

Paige remained strangely silent.

At that moment Dutch swung below. His big frame always looked oversize entering the salon. "Mind boiling up those bugs?" he asked.

Paige turned, chin quivering. She blinked back tears. "I had supper ready two hours ago—or doesn't anyone care about that? Am I the only one who cares if we have a family anymore?" She struggled to keep her voice steady.

Koby looked down. Every night her parents started arguing like this.

"Oh, I just thought we could fix these, too." Dutch squeezed Koby's shoulders. "Don't you agree, mate?"

Koby kept her head down. She didn't want to take sides—this wasn't about the lobsters or supper.

In icy silence Paige began boiling water. Dutch ducked forward briefly into Koby's V-berth, then headed aft to clean up.

"Is your schoolwork done?" Paige asked, glancing up with a raised eyebrow.

"Yeah." Koby turned away from her mom's stare.

"Why don't you show me."

"Don't you believe me?"

"Go get it and show me. Hurry, before we eat."

"I'm not hungry!" Koby said. "I can do my homework at school—I have study hall."

Paige wiped her hands on a towel and raised her voice. "Listen, young lady, I'm thinking of keeping your dinghy tied up for a few weeks until you learn to come home and do your homework. I'm tired of always worrying about you."

"Then don't!" Koby said. "Besides, Dad needs help pulling lobster traps."

"He gets by fine without us." Paige spoke plenty loud for Dutch to hear.

Not wearing her leggy, Koby hopped to her cabin and slammed the door. She threw herself on the triangular bunk. Her dinghy, *Titmouse*, was the one thing in life that kept the sailboat from becoming a floating prison. What was the big deal about coming home late? Ever since the accident, Mom had worried about her like she was a helpless baby. Well, if that helpless baby could save two whales, she could take care of herself, Koby thought.

Out in the salon, Dutch and Paige had begun arguing in muffled tones. Koby tried to cover her ears and block out the sound. Soon a loud knock sounded on her cabin door.

"Are you joining us?" Dutch called.

"No!" Koby said.

"What's wrong, mate?"

Koby didn't answer. Everything was wrong. Did he expect

her to be happy? Happy she had parents who argued all the time? Happy she was missing a foot? As she rolled over, her head hit a hard lump in the pillow. She opened the pillowcase. Inside, wrapped in a plastic bag, was the cobia's head she had saved for crab bait.

FIVE

"Oh, gross!" Koby squealed, dropping the bagged fish head. Then she giggled. Ever since moving aboard last year, she and Dad had been pulling these pranks: nudging each other overboard, lacing shoes with soggy spaghetti. Dad even ran her leggy up the mast once.

This fish head was Dad's way of getting back for the knots Koby had tied yesterday in his pant legs—which was payback for him knotting her shoelaces. Quietly Koby stood and opened the hatch to the top deck. She eased the square window open on its hinges. The boat rocked lightly as she placed the bag with the fish head up on the deck. She had a plan. Before crawling topside, she pulled on her insert and leggy, then grabbed a Magic Marker off the bookshelf. She squirmed quickly through the tight opening.

A fresh breeze greeted her. That meant the waves were probably choppy out on Chissom Reef. She hoped Lady and Squirt were all right. Koby breathed the sea air deeply and listened to the harbor sounds that she loved: waves slapping the hull, the clinking of the long halyards against the mast, the faint humming of other boats' generators. Out here, sirens and people's voices were only distant echoes. There were no loud noises except when her parents argued.

Silently Koby crept aft to the cockpit. She removed the fish head from the bag and placed it on the dash, beside the compass. The big cobia's head already had a strong fishy smell. By morning it would be crusty and foul.

In a drawer near the helm, Koby found a pair of Dad's sunglasses. She placed them carefully on the slimy head. Stifling a giggle, she drew a big mustache over the mouth with the Magic Marker. From the same drawer, she took out her dad's pipe. She positioned it in the cobia's stiff crusty lips. It looked great!

Grinning at her handiwork, Koby grabbed the Magic Marker and headed toward the rail. The two dinghies bumped gently against the hull. She moved carefully. Even wearing tennis shoes, it was hard to keep her leggy from sounding on the deck. On a Fiberglas boat, voices did not carry well between rooms. But sounds against the hull traveled the length of the boat like electricity. Koby remembered once sitting in her V-berth and tapping on the hull with a penny. For an hour her parents had searched the boat, looking for the noise.

Carefully, Koby crawled over the railing and eased down into her dad's dinghy. She opened up the air valve that kept the seat inflated. On the rubber surrounding the open valve, she drew a big happy face. She giggled and crawled back aboard, moving quietly forward to her favorite spot on the sailboat—a narrow wood platform jutting from the bow out over the water. This bow pulpit held the anchor and had a waist-high railing. Koby lowered herself into a sitting position and dangled her feet over the edge. Her stomach growled from not eating, but she would rather starve than sit at the table with Mom and Dad arguing. Or, worse yet, eating in silence.

The echo of music and hearty laughter drifted across the waves from other boats. Those sounds never came from *Dream Chaser*. Not anymore. Perched on the bow pulpit, Koby pretended she was out at sea. The black water slapping rhythmically at the hull and the breeze in her face made her feel free.

Maybe living on a sailboat wouldn't be so bad if they were always out at sea, she thought. Maybe then her parents wouldn't quarrel. At sea, life became magical. Once a huge manta ray had glided under the boat, its wings rising and falling as if flying. Often dolphins appeared like ghosts from the smoky blue deep, darting helter-skelter over the bow waves, rolling within inches of Koby's wiggling toes. Whales had breached clear of the water, crashing on their sides like thunder—sometimes so close they splashed the boat.

The ocean showed off. It had different moods and feelings, much like a person. Some days it rested, calm and peaceful. Other days great waves as big as toolsheds rose and fell. Once in a while it seemed that monsters were twisting under the dark and angry surface. A hurricane, Koby thought, must be an ocean throwing a temper tantrum. It made her wonder what she would be like if she were an ocean. She shook her head— her waves would be as big as mountains.

The breeze gusted harder, and Koby thought again of Lady and Squirt. Dad had said he'd go out with her in the morning.

This time she planned on holding him to his word. But what if they couldn't find the whales? Would that mean they had died?

A sound in the dark caused Koby to turn her head. Her parents were aft, climbing topside to the cockpit. They spoke in low tones, unaware of her sitting forward on the bow pulpit.

"Who knows," sounded Dutch's voice. "Maybe she did help a whale give birth."

"You'd believe her if she said she'd found Atlantis," Paige said.

"You never know."

"Quit it, Dutch! She disobeys, and you stick up for her. No whale would let her near its calf! And you don't help a plug cent, pretending to believe her."

"I'll install a truth meter on her," Dutch said with a faint chuckle. "Shouldn't be much harder than putting a gas gauge on a boat."

"I'm serious!"

"Oh, take it easy on our little mate. She *has* to learn to take care of herself. Besides, it's me you're mad at, not her."

"That little mate is growing up without a father, without a conscience, without discipline. Every day I worry she might drown out there somewhere."

"At least she'll drown having fun. You can't keep her locked up just because she's lost a foot."

"If I have to, I'll ground her before she kills herself. Dutch, you're no better than she is."

Koby nearly laughed at the thought of being grounded on water. Beached or stranded, maybe.

"I'm gone late 'cause I'm out pulling traps or at the docks

building more. Dang it, Paige, I'm trying to make the payments on this tub! Don't fight me."

"Last month's payment," Paige said. "You promised me this would be exciting. You talked me into moving out of a perfectly good house. For what? So we could sit anchored in this harbor? It seems as if all I do is clean, fix, and polish this boat."

"You can go ashore."

"Dutch, we have no telephone or TV. You moor out here in the harbor to save slip fees. How else are you going to save money—rent out the dinghies?"

"I'll put out more lobster traps," Dutch said stiffly.

"So you can lose more when boats run over the buoys? You've already lost nearly five hundred this year. Dutch, admit it: we can't afford to live this way."

"You'd love to sell *Dream Chaser*, wouldn't you?"

"It wouldn't be the end of the world to move back ashore."

Dutch spoke louder, his voice hard and deliberate. "And be stuck in some rat-infested apartment with neighbors screaming and fighting next door. Do you want a landlord stopping by each month to collect rent? Is that worth having your precious phone and cable TV?"

Paige started to speak, but he interrupted her. "For God's sake, can't you see? Out here nobody owns us! I can pull anchor tomorrow and sail away."

"Sure, and leave behind two thousand lobster traps. You talk as if Koby doesn't have school. As if you don't have a mortgage on this boat." Paige pointed ashore. "Face it—you might as well be anchored to the boathouse."

"Living ashore isn't the same," Dutch said, his voice hard. "Give me a couple more months; I'll make ends meet."

"Take as long as you want," Paige said, her voice growing cold and quiet. "Tomorrow, I'm taking Koby and moving ashore."

SIX

Koby sat suddenly upright and stared out across the black and troubled water. Hot tears burned in her eyes. What was Mom talking about, moving ashore?

Dutch stood, coughing roughly. "Paige, you'll do what you please. You always do!"

Paige did not answer.

A thick and uncomfortable silence blanketed the deck. Koby could not stop her tears—they came like waves pushing ashore. This was all her fault. Even with insurance, her accident had cost thousands of dollars. After the hospital, there had been therapy and the cost of fitting and refitting her artificial leg. Some of the bills still hadn't been paid.

Koby clenched her fists. If it helped, she'd quit fishing, quit taking out the dinghy. She would do her homework. She'd even grow a new foot, if only she could.

Dutch moved heavily to the companionway and swung down. Paige remained, staring out into the dark. Finally she stood stiffly and headed below. Her dark, shadowed movements looked jerky and slow. Long after the cabin doors clicked shut, Koby kept her seat on the bow pulpit.

How had this happened? It wasn't that her parents had never argued before. In fact, it often seemed as if that's all they did. That was why last year the idea of living on a boat had been so exciting. Koby thought it might make everybody happy. It might make everybody stop arguing.

At first it worked. Everybody helped to fix up the used sailboat and make it home. Working together had been fun. Every weekend they went sailing as a family and ate suppers on deck. But slowly that changed. Dad spent more and more time aboard his lobster boat, the *Lazy Mae*, trying to keep up with bills. Mom stayed aboard *Dream Chaser* doing maintenance and paperwork for dad. Koby swore there was more work to keeping a fifty-foot sailboat shipshape than to owning a castle, with all the varnishing, polishing, scrubbing, washing, scraping, and whatnot.

The arguments started again: small ones at first, then bigger ones. Koby hated the arguments about her medical bills. She hated it even worse when whole days passed without her parents speaking to each other. Sometimes Koby wondered if everyone would be better off if she just ran away. She stared out across the water, angry. The whole crummy world was coming unraveled.

She sat on the bow pulpit until she felt drained of all her feelings and tears. Lights had blinked off around the harbor. One by one the distant droning of boat generators stopped, and noises faded away onshore. Koby stood at last. How long she had sat perched out over the water, she didn't know. She retreated down the hatch and collapsed on the bunk. Questions clogged her brain.

All night Koby tossed with fitful dreams of being alone and abandoned. She dreamed of sharks circling closer and closer around a helpless whale and calf. Their razor teeth glinted wickedly. When suddenly one flashed in and struck viciously at the calf, Koby woke with a start. Sweat beaded her forehead. The air in the V-berth breathed stuffy like thick smoke. She reached up and opened the darkened hatch. Dawn's gray light was starting to soften the inky black sky.

Topside, a nervous breeze shifted over the deck. The stars blinked dimly through a haze. Koby wondered how Lady and Squirt had spent the night. Were they even alive? As she lay sweating on the clammy sheet, her anger returned. Mom's simple sentence, "I'm taking Koby and moving ashore," had turned the world upside down.

Koby sat up and dressed. Pulling on her windbreaker, she slipped from the V-berth into the main salon. The darkness forced her to grope her way to the galley, where she filled a pocket with cookies and guzzled milk directly from the plastic jug in the refrigerator. Quietly she tiptoed back to her parents' master berth in the stern. They slept soundly. She shook her dad's arm. "Wake up," she whispered.

Dutch stirred and rolled away.

Koby reached and pinched his nose closed.

He snorted and coughed and sat up, brushing her hand aside.

"It's time," she said.

"For what?" he sputtered.

"To look for the whales."

Dutch rubbed his eyes and pressed his hands to his head as if cradling a bad headache. "Ah, c'mon, you're not serious?"

"Hurry, you promised!"

Paige raised her head and mumbled, "What's going on?"

"We're going out to look for the whales," Koby said.

"What time is it?"

Koby ignored the question. "I'll get the dinghy started."

"It's barely light out!" Dutch grumbled.

"That's why we have to get going." Koby turned and headed from the master berth. "In two minutes I'm filling your boots with crab bait," she called. She smiled when she heard the loud clunk of her dad's feet hitting the wooden floor. This wouldn't have been the first time she stuffed his rubber boots with guts and fish heads.

By the time Dutch shuffled topside, Koby had her dinghy running. She raced the motor impatiently. Dutch came to the rail, his hair and beard matted. "Let's take mine," he called gruffly. "It's faster."

"The seat's flat," Koby shouted.

He gave his dinghy a look of disgust as he crawled aboard *Titmouse* and cast off.

Koby idled quickly from Pelican Harbor. This morning her stump was sore, but she kept her leggy on. After clearing the moored boats, she opened the throttle wide until she banked into Colter's Cut. *Titmouse* handled sluggishly with two people aboard. The water stretched flat and smooth like glass. A hazy mist blurred the dawn sky.

Koby ate cookies from her pocket as she steered. Taking Colter's Cut in daylight was a breeze, she thought, glancing at her dad. He looked tired and kept his gaze leveled forward across the bow.

Over Lonesome Key a dull red glow warmed the horizon. Koby swallowed another dry mouthful of cookie as she veered back and forth through the mangroves. Daydreaming, she swerved sharply to miss a floating stump.

"Watch where you're going!" Dutch grumped.

Koby steered more carefully.

As they cleared the cut, moderate swells and two-foot choppy waves greeted them. Even inside the reef, the ocean looked restless. *Titmouse* splashed along, rising and falling in the swells. Though relaxed, a deep sadness filled Dutch's distant gaze.

Three miles offshore a line of heavier swells and white-capped waves marked where the water deepened beyond the underwater coral of Chissom Reef. Koby braced herself and squinted. It was hard to tell exactly where the whales had been the night before. Maybe they had moved. She slowed and idled in circles.

"Where do you think they are?" she asked Dutch.

"Beats me, you're the one who saw them."

Koby searched. "It was out past the flats," she said, referring to the shallow sea grass meadows near shore.

"Was it inside the reef?"

Koby nodded. "I threw anchor." Outside the reef she knew it was too deep to anchor. "I should be able to see Squirt's splashes," she said.

Dutch studied her with a peculiar look. "Squirt?"

"Yeah, that's what I named the baby. The mom is Lady."

Dutch shook his head but did not answer. He scanned the waves with a hardened stare, his mouth drawn in a tight line.

After crisscrossing the water in silence for nearly an hour, Dutch motioned. "These waves and swells make it hard. Are you sure you saw them?"

Koby turned angrily. "You and Mom really don't believe me, do you?"

"I meant that waves can play tricks on your eyes."

Koby grabbed a strand of tangled netting from the dinghy floor. "You think I swam up and cut this off a wave?"

Dutch did not answer.

Koby kept circling, searching desperately. Finally Dutch motioned toward the bright horizon. "We better get back. You have school."

"Can't we look just a little longer?"

"Not now, maybe later."

"Yeah, I know, maybe never," Koby said. Purposely she swerved hard toward home. Dutch braced his hand against the side and looked back. Koby kept gazing toward shore. The outboard whined loudly.

"If you saw them, I believe you," Dutch shouted. He placed his hand on her shoulder and squeezed lightly.

Koby ignored the squeeze and watched the blur of water

passing under the bow. Not until they entered the harbor did either one speak.

"I've got to work my lobster traps today, mate," Dutch said. "But if I'm in early, we'll try again."

"You never get home early," Koby said, pulling alongside *Dream Chaser*. She crawled quickly aboard the sailboat. She wanted to ask if he and Mom were really splitting up. And why. But she dared not let on that she'd been listening.

"Hey, mate!"

Koby glanced back.

Dutch winked. He paused as if he wanted to say something, but finally coughed. "Here." He handed her the bowline. "Get your bones ready for school."

Koby cleated the line tightly and headed down the companionway. In the galley, Paige had coffee brewing and breakfast set out. "So, did you find your whales?" she asked.

"Would you believe me if I did?"

"Honey, don't you realize how crazy this whole thing sounds?"

"I'll find them," Koby said.

Paige sat watching her in awkward silence. Koby wolfed down her sourdough waffles. Everyone could believe what they wanted, she thought. It wouldn't stop her from looking.

Finishing breakfast, Koby headed for the V-berth. Quickly she jerked off the leggy and sponged her stump clean. Then she dried it and dusted it with powder. Next she pulled on a dry tube sock. Today her stump was swollen so she wore a thinner pair of socks. Usually she wore much thicker ones to make her leggy fit snugly. After checking to make sure there were no wrinkles, she slid on the worn insert. Last, she pushed into the leggy.

Before dressing, Koby brushed back her long brown hair and looked into the mirror on the door. She could see herself from the waist up. In some ways she looked like Mom. Her arms were tanned and strong, her hair sun bleached. But there were changes taking place in Koby's body. Some of these changes she could see; they excited her and embarrassed her. But there were other changes. Ones inside. These nobody could see or understand. Koby did not understand them herself. They were feelings that frightened her and made her feel alone. Often she wanted to laugh and at the same time cry.

"You're going to miss the school bus," Paige called, knocking on the door.

Koby stopped her daydreaming and pulled on a T-shirt, jeans, and tennis shoes. Other kids wore shorts here in the Keys, but Koby would rather die than have everybody see her stump or her phony leggy.

"Are you ready?" Paige called again.

"Yes, Mom!" Koby shouted. She poked out her tongue at the mirror and opened the door.

"Here's your lunch, sweetheart," Paige said softly, her voice cracking. Suddenly she hugged Koby. "Just know I love you, darling. No matter what."

"I love you, too," Koby said, hugging Paige. Part of her wanted to hug forever. Another part of her was angry at Mom. Finally she let go. Lunch bag in hand, she climbed topside.

"Honey, after school I want to talk to you."

"I'm going to look for the whales," Koby called. She ignored the hurt silence as she headed for *Titmouse*.

Dutch waved good-bye from the bow. Koby waved back. He probably hadn't even noticed the fish head or the happy face on the flat seat, she thought. Reaching to untie the dinghy, she stopped. The line was knotted two feet down with half hitches.

Dutch called over with a big smile, "Need help?"

"It's not funny, Dad!" Koby yelled. "I have to catch the school bus."

"Go ahead and take my dinghy," Dutch said. "Unless you don't like sitting on flat seats."

Angrily Koby grabbed a knife from the cockpit and cut the line, leaving the two-foot section of knots hanging.

Dutch walked over, a stern look on his face. "Don't get snorty, mate!" he said sharply. "Lines don't grow on trees."

Koby jumped into *Titmouse* and pushed off. "I won't need it living onshore!"

"Onshore?" Dutch said, his voice quiet. "You heard—"

Koby jerked the cord on the outboard and let the engine's roar drown his voice. Gunning the throttle, she raced toward the dock. It didn't matter if the wake sank a battleship.

SEVEN

Koby tied off quickly to the dock and rushed to catch the bus already screeching to a stop in the parking lot. She saw her old friend Nickeljack by the boathouse and waved—she needed to talk to him after school.

Breathing hard, she climbed aboard and searched for an empty seat. Seldom did anyone save her one. The other kids treated her as if she had a dreaded disease, especially the boys. They acted as if they would lose a foot, too, if they sat next to her.

It hadn't always been this way. Not before the accident. But when she returned to school after leaving the hospital, she had been in a wheelchair until she could be fitted with an artificial foot. Right away almost everyone started avoiding her. She didn't care. She didn't feel much like talking to anyone, anyway. Besides, what was there to talk about when you had a foot missing?

That was why Koby loved the ocean and why she loved the night. In her dreams and in that neverland between asleep and awake, she could play, running faster than the wind. In that dream space she could escape all the hurt—the unfairness.

As the bus pulled up to school, Koby felt more alone than ever. Even a close friend probably wouldn't understand about the whales or be able to do anything about Mom and Dad.

After a quick stop at her locker, Koby headed to her first class, history. The hour lasted forever, as did study hall and then science. Koby found herself staring out the window, thinking about her mom and dad, and about Squirt and Lady.

After lunch came PE class, Koby's most dreaded hour. She entered the locker room, head hung low. The other girls ran around half naked, screaming and changing clothes. As usual, Koby huddled alone in the corner. Quickly she squirmed into her sweatpants—she was the only girl in the class not wearing shorts. She peeked back and caught one of the girls, Becky Norman, watching her.

Koby pretended not to notice. Becky's clothes, her looks, her walk, her voice, her long hair—everything about her was perfect. All the girls copied whatever Becky Norman did. Right now Becky was staring.

"Everyone outside as soon as you're ready!" shouted Mrs. Hurley, the teacher. "Today we're playing soccer!"

Koby walked slowly, avoiding all the jostling. She hated school sports. She could balance and hop well, and she could dive and swim. But that didn't seem to matter. She was always the last to be picked for any team. Today was no different.

When the game finally ended, everyone ran inside to shower. Koby hung behind. She checked to see that nobody was watching, then splashed a little water on her hair. Now it looked as if she had showered. She would rather die and rot than hop naked into the shower with her stump showing.

The bell rang.

As Koby left the locker room, she came face-to-face with Becky. Quickly she looked down and walked past.

When finally the day's last buzzer rang, Koby rushed from the school and plopped herself into the front seat of the waiting bus. She ignored the usual shouting and yelling as she rode. She needed to speak to Nickeljack.

When the bus arrived at the harbor, Koby jumped off. Her old friend was sitting on the seawall, a shrimp net draped over his lap. His gnarled fingers tugged at the shimmering blanket of blue, mending holes and breaks. At his side slept Squid, his overweight basset hound.

Nickeljack was a retired sea captain who worked odd jobs around the harbor. The bent old man drank quick swallows of whiskey from a small bottle in his pocket whenever he thought nobody was watching. His dark skin hung loose on his bony body. Once Koby had asked him why his name was Nickeljack. He grumbled almost angrily, "It's better than Dollar Bill!"

Most boat owners treated Nickeljack as if he were a bum unless they had a dirty job for him. Even Mom and Dad didn't trust him. Nickeljack's hooded eyes had a mysterious, angry look. He glared at people and snarled when he talked. Halfway through a sentence he'd stop and wave someone away as if they were too dumb to spit.

Still, Koby liked the old man. He never seemed to notice her leggy, and he always listened to her and told her secret fishing spots. Around her, he allowed a laugh in his voice. The glare in his eyes melted.

As Koby approached the seawall, Charlie, the local great white heron, strutted toward her. His yellow spindly legs looked as if they were made of plastic. Koby knew how that felt. From her lunch bag she pulled a piece of bread she'd saved. She tossed it, and the bird snapped it up. Stretching his neck, he swallowed.

Nickeljack's fat basset hound struggled to his feet and waddled toward her, his stomach barely clearing the ground. She ran and dropped to her knees. "How you doing, Squid?" She dug in her lunch bag for another treat. Every day she saved something from her lunch for Charlie and Squid. "Did you miss me, huh?" she cooed, scratching the plump dog under the chin.

"He always misses you," Nickeljack said coarsely, looking up. "No one else treats him like a real dog."

"You're the best pooch in the whole world," she said, scratching the hound's long ears.

"Good for fish bait," Nickeljack said gruffly.

Koby laughed. She knew Nickeljack loved Squid. In fact, the old captain loved all animals. It was people that made him grumpy. Squid rubbed against Koby's knees, finally rolling over to have his belly scratched.

"Sure got you trained," Nickeljack muttered.

Koby laughed and stood.

Nickeljack pointed down the seawall. "That Charlie won't let anyone 'cept you get close."

"I always have food."

He shook his head. "No, lots of people got food. Animals know things 'bout people."

Koby chuckled. "He knows I'm a sucker."

"Even I know that. What got you up so early? I saw you and Dutch leave at first light."

"Yesterday I found a hurt whale. We went out looking for her." Koby described the animal.

"Sounds like a pilot whale," Nickeljack said. "How bad was she hurt?"

Koby eyed the net on Nickeljack's lap. "She was caught in a net like that one. Almost killed her. How come you fix those things for people?"

Nickeljack held up a handful of weave. "People blame the nets, but it ain't this that kills things."

"What do you mean?"

"It's the people that don't bother freeing a net when it snags on a reef. Or the slugs who throw the nets overboard when they get patchy. They's the ones that kill the whales and the dolphins. It ain't the nets!" When she didn't answer, he raised an eyebrow. "So, what about this whale you found?"

She told about cutting the net off and all about the calf and bringing it to the surface. Nickeljack stared out at the ocean, listening intently as she spoke. "While the calf was playing," she finished, "I swam right up to the mom and touched her. I petted her face."

Nickeljack frowned. Without warning he turned and reached out. He rubbed his gnarly hand roughly across her forehead.

Surprised and frightened, Koby drew back.

He smiled. "If you don't like it, how come you did it to the whale? Let animals do the first touchin'."

"But she was hurt!"

"Even more reason."

Koby nodded but remained back a step. "Anyway, this morning we went looking for them."

"Did you find 'em?"

Koby shook her head. "Maybe the sharks got them?"

Nickeljack gazed at the ocean, his face expressionless. His eyes grew blank, and for several minutes he sat in his trancelike state. Finally he blinked. A peaceful look melted over his face. "They're out there—the sharks ain't found 'em."

"How do you know?" Koby asked doubtfully.

He smiled thinly, his eyes suddenly warm. "I know, 'cause last night I slept good. I don't usually sleep much at all."

"What does sleeping have to do with whales?" Koby asked. "Have you been drinking?"

Nickeljack's cheeks relaxed. "A heart don't get drunk. . . . I wish it could." He continued to tie the delicate nylon strands of the net with his bony fingers. The blue-tinted mesh draped from his knees like a dress. He frowned. "By the way, you didn't tie off *Titmouse* very good this morning. I went down after you left and snugged her up." He jerked firmly at a knot in the net. "People do fine in life if all the knots they tie is good."

"And if they have both feet," Koby added.

Nickeljack raised an eyebrow and studied her as if she were a puzzle. "I reckon as how everyone's got somethin' wrong with them."

"Not like me!"

"You're right, all you're missing is a little chunk of leg. That ain't of much account." Nickeljack pointed to his heart. "Most people have their hurts in here. Inside hurts don't fix as easy."

"So, what's wrong with you?"

"Maybe I didn't learn to laugh enough."

"What's there to laugh about?"

Nickeljack whistled low. "Heavens, girl, did you swallow an anchor? There's more than whales on your mind."

"No, I'm just thinking about the whales."

Nickeljack raised a crooked finger. "There's more, and you can tell me about it when you want." He made a gruesome face. "Until then it'll rot your innards."

Koby shifted awkwardly on her feet, kicking at the dirt. Head down, she spoke quietly. "Mom is leaving Dad. She's moving ashore and taking me with her."

Nickeljack jerked extra hard on a knot, then raised the net to his mouth and nipped off a stub of line with his teeth. "Dutch and Paige, I always figured their knot was loose."

"What can I do?"

"Maybe nothin'."

For several long minutes Nickeljack kept working in silence. "So," he finally grunted, "are you going looking for the whales again?"

Koby nodded. "As soon as I change clothes."

"Be sure to think the way they think."

"Nickeljack, I'm not a fish."

"Sometimes I wonder. Besides, whales ain't fish. They bleed warm blood and get scared and lonely just like you. Even breathe the same air."

"I know that, but I'm not a whale, either."

Nickeljack shook his head patiently. "You're a Conch. Do you know what that means?"

"Yeah, means I was born here in the Keys."

"Being born here's only half of it. You think different than the tourists and the landlubbers. I've watched you play in the water since you was smaller than Squid."

"I'm still smaller than him," Koby said, grinning.

Nickeljack did not smile. "You aren't afraid of the water. Not a lick afraid."

"But that doesn't mean I think like a whale."

"The ocean don't care if you got scales, fins, toes, or stumps. If you plan on helping the whales, you *have* to feel and think like them."

"I don't understand what you're saying," Koby said, turning to leave. "I have to get going. Do you want to come along?"

Nickeljack shook his head and rolled his lips in thought. "You're the one hurting inside, so you best go alone."

"I'm not hurting inside!"

Nickeljack did not answer.

Koby left, shaking her head—sometimes she wondered if others were right about the old man. Not until she reached the dinghy did Nickeljack call after her with his croaky voice.

"Koby, you listen to your heart . . . and take good care of yourself."

She smiled as she waved. This was a little game she had going with Nickeljack. Together they shouted, "'Cause nobody else will!"

EIGHT

Koby puzzled as she motored out to *Dream Chaser*. What did Nickeljack mean, "Listen to your heart"? As she approached the boat, Dutch poked his head up from the cabin and waved. Koby waved back, surprised. Dad was never back early unless the wind was tying knots in his shoelaces.

"Are you going to look for the whales?" he called.

Koby climbed aboard. "Yup, as soon as I grab my stuff."

Dutch stepped topside. "I think your mother wants to talk to you first."

"About what?"

"I think you know."

Koby bit at her lip and went below deck.

Paige looked up as Koby arrived. On the floor were bags and suitcases already packed. Paige wiped her hands on a towel and walked over. "Your father said you heard us talking last night." She took Koby by the shoulders and drew her close.

Koby pulled away.

"Why didn't you say something this morning?" Paige asked.

"Why didn't you?"

Paige started to argue but stopped. "Your father and I need to be apart, at least for a while."

"Don't you care about me?"

"Oh, honey, it has nothing to do with you."

"That's obvious!" Koby said. "So, where are you going?"

"It will be *us*, honey. You know Tess Morgan—she offered to let us stay with her over on oceanside."

"What will you do for money?"

"Ed Baines will let me do some secretary work at the marina office. It won't be much, but it's something. Most of your stuff is packed, but you need to look around."

"Can't I stay here?"

"With your father gone so much, that won't work."

In a weird sort of way, Koby wanted to laugh. Yesterday her parents had been Dutch and Paige to each other. Now they talked about each other as "your mother" or "your father," as if each were Koby's responsibility.

"Nobody ever asks me what I want," she said.

"I'm sorry. Now go look around before we leave."

"Mom, I'm going to look for the whales."

"No, not now, we need to get moved. Maybe tomorrow."

Koby's insides burned with anger. She knew now how helpless the whale had felt, caught in a shrimp net. She was in her own net, an invisible one knotted up with her parents' bitterness, selfishness, and silly pride. Neither Mom nor Dad ever tried to be nice to each other. All they cared about was themselves.

"Hurry up now and look around," Paige said.

Koby set her chin with a deep breath. "No!" she said. "You don't really care about me or the whales."

Paige turned, surprised. "Young lady, it's not your choice. We're going to . . ." Her look suddenly melted. "Oh, honey, we can't be fighting. Not now. We need each other." She hugged Koby again.

"I'll go to Tess's if you let me look for the whales," Koby said.

Paige kept hugging Koby so hard it hurt. Finally she let go and nodded. "I'll pick you up at the dock at eight o'clock sharp. That will give you four hours, okay?"

Koby nodded.

"Remember, eight o'clock. And be careful," Paige said.

After slipping into her swimsuit and grabbing a windbreaker, Koby rushed topside to board *Titmouse*. She brought along a pair of binoculars.

Dutch was preparing to scale the mast to change a mast light that had burned out. "Want to go up?" he asked, motioning.

Koby loved being hoisted up in the bosun's chair. She hesitated. "I have to go look for the whales."

"Wait up a minute; I'll go along," he said.

Right now Koby wanted to be alone. She shook her head. "No, Dad. I have to go alone."

"Why?"

She shrugged. Trying to explain what Nickeljack had said wouldn't have made a lick of sense.

"Okay, do what you want," he said, rubbing his thick white beard.

Rushing, Koby untied *Titmouse* and motored from the harbor. Once clear of the other boats, she reached down and pulled off her leggy and insert, then twisted the throttle hard. She was free! Soon the mangroves blurred as she weaved through the cut. In ten minutes she bounced onto open ocean toward the reef. The water had a lighter chop now. Luckily there were no swells—swells made the water hilly. For half an hour she kept the throttle wide open, searching back and forth between the reef and shore.

Except for occasional whitecaps, nothing interrupted the scalloped waves. Finally Koby idled to a stop and pulled out the binoculars. The whales could be anywhere. She glassed around slowly. The ocean kept playing tricks on her. Each time something broke the waves' endless pattern, it turned out to be floating debris or her imagination.

Finally Koby rested the binoculars on her lap and rubbed her weary eyes. Nickeljack had said, "If you plan on helping the whales, you *have* to feel and think like them."

Koby figured that if she was hurt she would want help. She imagined a whale in a thirty-foot-long hospital bed, watching TV. That wasn't what Nickeljack had meant. But what if there was no help? Again she puzzled. She would go someplace safe— maybe that's what Nickeljack meant. But where would a whale feel safe?

She kept scanning the waves—the surface all looked the same. She knew that nearer to shore the sea grass flats stretched like underwater meadows. Farther west the meadows ran up against the sand flats, both too shallow for a whale to dive from danger. Out here, the coral reef guarded the shoreline like a jagged underwater wall. Sharks often cruised the reefs, feeding on schools of fish. Beyond the reef stretched deep open water. That didn't seem safe, either.

The only other place nearby was the Cumberland Banks. This large underwater channel snaked in through the shallow sand flats at the west end. There wouldn't be much to eat in the channel, but often she had seen dolphins resting near the banks. She had never seen sharks there.

Koby debated all the choices. Nickeljack had said to listen to her heart. All it was doing was going *thump-thump, thump-thump.* He had also said that if she planned on helping the whales she had to feel and think like them. She closed her eyes and imagined herself as a mother whale, her flipper gashed, her body battered. She also imagined a helpless whale calf frolicking beside her. If night was coming and sharks were prowling the waters, where would she go? Where? Where? Opening her eyes, she revved the engine and headed westward toward the Cumberland Banks.

The water remained a shimmering green over the grass flats until the bottom turned to sand. Then it turned to pale gray. When the gray darkened into a deep blue, Koby killed the engine. This was the channel.

Patiently she glassed the waves between *Titmouse* and the horizon. By kneeling her stump on the side, she could stand and see better. If there were whales, they would have to surface soon to breathe. Then she might spot the misty chuffs of their blows.

Something flickered in the distance. Koby squinted but could not penetrate the sun's sharp reflection. She started the engine. By angling a few hundred yards toward shore, she avoided the bright glare.

Stopping once more, she raised the binoculars to her eyes. What had she seen? She scanned the waves, her gaze sweeping downward from the horizon. Still nothing.

And then they appeared.

A large dorsal fin broke the waves, followed immediately by a small one. Koby lowered the binoculars. The fins could be seen clearly. They were whales. From this distance, though, it was hard to tell—was it Lady and Squirt?

NINE

Koby reached to start the outboard, then stopped. If it was Lady and Squirt, she didn't want to spook them. They were moving this way. Heart skipping, Koby dropped the anchor overboard. The line played out loop after loop like a snake. If the anchor didn't reach bottom, even a slack tide would drift the dinghy. With one coil left the line relaxed.

"Good!" Koby breathed.

Quickly she pulled on her single fin and mask. The whales continued to roll across the waves toward her. The large one rose and dropped sluggishly. The calf broke the waves with frisky leaps and tail slaps. Koby eased into the water. She worked her fin, gliding gently away from *Titmouse*, arms at her side. Still, it was hard to tell if the two were Lady and Squirt.

The whales had closed to within a hundred feet. Reflections on the choppy water blurred their movements. Koby swam directly into their path. The mother slowed, then floated to a stop a stick's throw away. The calf had vanished.

As a lazy breeze ruffled the waves, Koby fought the urge to move forward—she remembered Nickeljack's words when he rubbed her face with his bony hand. Suddenly an eerie feeling spread over Koby. It was as if something had crept up on her in the dark. She glanced back. Nothing. Drawing a breath, she dipped her mask for a look. That instant an underwater current made the water boil. The calf burst free of the surface within arm's reach. Puffing, he spun and flipped wildly, hit the water, and disappeared.

Koby came up sputtering and laughing. "You little sneak!"

Suddenly her laughter turned to horror. The mother was swimming in. Faster and faster she came, attacking! Koby jerked her knees up to ward off the impact—she knew whales killed sharks by ramming them. The mother whale veered at the last second, her wake flipping Koby backward. Her tail fluke smashed the water; her black eyes blazed.

Salt spray stung Koby's cheeks and filled her mouth. She coughed and choked, trying to keep her head up. The whale floated only yards away. "Eeeasy, Lady. Eeeeasy," Koby gasped, blinking back tears. She recognized the deep gash on Lady's right flipper. The edges were puffy white, and the raw cut still gaped open. Koby's voice quavered when she spoke. "I won't hurt your baby."

Still Lady glared and made jaw-popping sounds.

Koby looked away from the angry eyes. She did not want her actions to seem like a challenge. "You remember me, *don't you?*" she pleaded.

Lady's sounds changed to sharp crackly buzzes, then high-pitched clicks. Koby swore she could feel the sound. Lady's sonar was sounding her. Suddenly the clicking stopped, and the harried look in Lady's eyes softened. Nearby the calf surfaced, chattering and squealing. Lady's gaze flickered toward her baby.

Softly, rhythmically, Koby cooed and talked. She kept her arms by her side.

Lady drifted away, then moved closer again.

"I won't hurt you, girl. That's it, easy now." Koby remembered Nickeljack telling her to feel and think like the whales. Her muscles tensed. She tried to relax, tilting her head sideways and smiling. "I knew you were alive," she whispered.

Lady's eyes glistened as she tossed her melon head side to side, whistling. Again she sounded a burst of clicks. With barely a twitch of her tail fluke, she glided within arm's reach and submerged her head. Koby felt a buzzing tingle in her stump. The rest of her body crawled with energy as if it were inches from an electric fence.

The buzzing stopped. Lady surfaced and turned sideways, keeping her wounded right flipper away from Koby.

"It's okay, Lady, I won't touch it."

Now Lady bumped against Koby for the first time. Koby looked at the whale's big glassy eyes. What feelings hid behind that gentle and haunting stare? she wondered. She reached, hesitantly, and slid her hand under the shiny dark body. It felt smoother than she remembered, almost warm. Lady let out a soft whistle.

"I'm so proud of you," Koby whispered. "You took care of Squirt." Remembering the calf, she looked and saw him circling. He clicked and squeaked, keeping his distance.

"He doesn't trust me," Koby said, stroking Lady gently.

The mother floated, motionless but alert.

"I'm not hurting your mom—don't be afraid," Koby called to the calf as she eased away from Lady. She put the snorkel in her mouth. Adjusting her mask, she drew two quick breaths and submerged.

Out of the hazy blue, Squirt came like a black torpedo, dodging and darting. He circled, then cut in. Koby twisted to face him. He flashed past and shot upward to disappear above the waves. Then he crashed back in with an explosion of bubbles. The sun cast an eerie glow through the white mist. Koby surfaced.

Squirt kept circling around Koby, splashing with clumsy leaps. Lady watched quietly.

"Here, Squirt," Koby called.

Squirt glided in like a shadow. Breaking the waves, he slapped his tail into a dive again. This time he streaked back around more quickly. At last he coasted within arm's reach and hovered still. His marble eyes glinted.

Koby smiled and slipped under again to look. The light-colored rings still showed around Squirt's body. He stretched his mouth open as if yawning. Then he came to life once more, twisting downward out of sight. Koby surfaced, breathing heavily. Lady remained nearby, keeping a watchful eye. Koby swam back beside her. "I'm beat!" she said.

The big whale seemed to know the play had ended. She whistled low. Squirt returned immediately to his mother's side, squeaking and whistling. Together they turned and headed away. A mix of happiness and sadness rushed through Koby's thoughts. When would she see her friends again?

Lady kept arching and rolling her back across the waves on a straight course out from shore. Squirt slipped from sight. Koby guessed they were headed toward the reef to eat before the sharks began their nighttime prowl. Winded, tired, but thrilled, Koby turned toward the dinghy. Squirt had not surfaced again.

Suddenly the water swirled. Something nudged Koby in the rump, bunting her up several inches. She flinched as the calf slapped his tail hard. He disappeared in a flash toward Lady.

"You turkey!" Koby gasped. She watched the calf join his mother. Soon the two disappeared among the distant waves.

Every inch of Koby's body smiled. She backstroked toward *Titmouse*, small waves breaking against her neck. Overhead a black frigate bird soared shoreward. Farther out, two pelicans dive-bombed the waves for fish—it was amazing that the crazy birds didn't get headaches. Koby smiled—life didn't get any better.

But then the thought struck her. Tonight she would not be sleeping aboard *Dream Chaser*. Tonight Mom would not be sleeping with Dad. Suddenly the water seemed cold.

TEN

Titmouse meandered along toward home. Koby had been alone in a magic bubble with Lady, Squirt, and the ocean. Now thoughts of her parents burst that bubble. A dark gloom, worse than any night shadow, filled the air. It swallowed her thoughts as she stared back out at the ocean. If only she could steer toward the horizon and never come back. Reluctantly she headed into Colter's Cut.

An eerie silence blanketed the twisting waterway. Even the birds were still, as if sharing her feelings. She continued. Soon she had navigated the cut, and the entrance to Pelican Harbor appeared. Koby took a deep breath and motored in.

On *Dream Chaser*, Dutch was stooped over, working on the deck. He spotted her and waved. Without waving back, Koby steered alongside and tied off. Slowly, deliberately, she pulled on her sock, insert, and leggy.

"Find 'em?" Dutch called.

Koby adjusted the leggy strap. "Yup."

Dutch looked surprised. "Well, how are they?"

"Okay, I guess. They were over in Cumberland Banks. Is Mom gone?"

Dutch nodded. He shuffled to the railing and gave her a hand up. Koby retreated to the V-berth and cleaned her stump, then pulled on jeans over her swimsuit. The V-berth was stripped of everything that showed it was hers. And it *was* hers. So was the bow pulpit. She returned to the salon and began gathering things her mom had forgotten in the main salon. Dutch watched quietly.

Koby found her teddy bear, dozens of shells, an old straw hat, and a small dried blowfish she had caught. She paused beside the table. "Can I just leave this stuff here for when I come back?"

Dutch fidgeted with his shirtsleeves. "I don't know what your mother has planned," he said.

"Dad, don't talk about Mom like she's a stranger."

Dutch met her gaze, his lips quivering and his eyes glassy. "I ain't leaving you stranded, mate," he blurted. "This is still your home, too, anytime you want."

Koby rushed desperately into his arms. The room blurred as she hugged her dad's broad chest and felt his strong arms grip her body. She wanted to be held forever and ever, but soon Dutch relaxed his hold. Koby let go and pushed away. "I-I'd better go—Mom's waiting," she stammered.

Dutch nodded and followed topside. As Koby crawled into the dinghy, Dutch loosened the bowline and pushed her free. "Here!" he said, tossing something in the air.

Before she could stop herself, Koby caught the smelly cobia head, now two days old. The black mustache still showed over the crusted top lip. "Yuck!" she said, dropping it into the water.

"Aw, shucks, thought you'd want to save it," he said.

Koby rinsed her hands without smiling. As she started the engine, Dutch hollered, "Don't forget where I live." She gunned the engine in response.

Halfway in, Koby spotted her mom waiting on the dock. She turned and looked back toward *Dream Chaser*. Dutch stood by the rail, watching. Suddenly the dinghy felt like a life raft adrift between two worlds. Hesitantly Koby approached the dock.

Paige called, "I think you'll like where we're staying."

Quietly, Koby tied off and climbed ashore. "I'll meet you at the car," she said, avoiding Paige's eyes. She headed toward Nickeljack, who sat on the seawall mending another shrimp net.

"Make it quick," Paige called.

Koby wished her parents trusted the old sea captain. All they saw were his sloppy clothes, gruffness, and whiskey bottle. They never gave him a chance.

"Sure got yourself a busy family today," Nickeljack grunted.

"What family?" Koby said.

Nickeljack rubbed his chin thoughtfully. "Did you find the whales?"

"Yeah! They swam right up to me." She didn't tell about the bluff charge. "The mom is still hurt bad. Her flipper is cut, and she won't dive."

"Maybe she wants your help."

"How can I help?"

Nickeljack shrugged. "I'll think on it. You run with your

mom now." He jerked hard on the weave to set a knot. "Knots are coming loose everywhere today," he muttered.

Koby broke into tears. "Nickeljack, Mom and Dad are breaking up because of me, aren't they!"

"Don't you ever think that," Nickeljack said severely. "Here, watch!" He reached down and picked up a length of rope. From his pocket, he pulled a fine piece of fishing line. He handed her both. "Tie me a good square knot," he ordered.

Koby started to protest, but she saw his chin stiffen. Awkwardly she looped the rope around the thin fishing line and formed a square knot.

Nickeljack reached and grabbed the ends and jerked them easily apart. "How come they didn't stay together?" he demanded.

"One's a big piece of rope, the other is thin fishing line," she said.

"Knots come loose for two reasons: they ain't tied right, or the lines is different."

"You think Mom and Dad are different, don't you?"

"I reckon it's possible. Just remember, whatever happens, you take good care of yourself." He raised a finger as if to direct a choir.

"*'Cause nobody else will!*" they chorused.

Koby smiled as she sniffled back tears.

Nickeljack nodded. "That's better; now go on. Come see me tomorrow."

"Why?"

He waved her away without looking up.

She wiped at her eyes as she headed for the parking lot.

"I worry about you talking to that guy," Paige said, as Koby climbed into the station wagon.

"He's my friend!" Koby said.

"That's what worries me. I'm not sure I trust him."

"Maybe he doesn't trust you, either."

"Honey, be nice."

"You be nice, too. Where we going?"

"I told you—to stay at Tess Morgan's. You'll like it."

"Do we have to live there?" Koby asked.

"We'll find our own apartment soon."

Koby stared out the window as trees and buildings flashed past. Tess lived on the northeast end of Lonesome Key, ocean-side. Her home was only four miles from Pelican Harbor, but it seemed a planet away.

"Can I keep *Titmouse* in Tess's canal?" Koby asked.

"We'll have to ask."

As they pulled to a stop in front of a small blue house, Koby spotted Tess Morgan stooped over in her yard trimming flowers. She was more than plump. She spotted them and rushed over. Before Koby could step from the car, Tess smothered her with a hug. "Oh, this is so exciting," she gushed. "It's like a big adventure! Tomorrow after school, we all *must* go to town and shop." She winked. "For girls' things, you know."

"I have to go see Lady and Squirt again," Koby mumbled.

"You have pets. Paige didn't tell me about them."

"They're whales."

Tess and Paige exchanged quiet glances. "Honey, you didn't tell me if you found the whales," Paige said.

"You didn't ask!"

A sharpness edged Paige's voice. "Now I'm asking."

Reluctantly Koby explained what had happened. Paige looked concerned. Before Koby finished, Tess grabbed her hand. "Sounds like quite the story. Let's show you to your room now." She started toward the house with Koby and Paige in tow.

By bedtime, Koby was crawling the walls. She swore Tess's mouth was plugged in. Tess carried on as if a family breaking up was a big trip to Disney World or something. "Oh, this is going to be so fun!" she kept saying. "I can't wait to introduce you to all the neighbors!" The final straw came when Tess clapped her hands and exclaimed, "I already feel like we're one big happy family!"

Koby burst into tears and ran down the darkened hallway to what was now her bedroom. She slammed the door and leaned against it as if a monster were trying to push it open. She was anything but happy, she thought. And Tess Morgan sure wasn't family.

Paige knocked. "Can we talk?" she called softly.

Koby did not answer. Soon Paige's footsteps disappeared down the hall. Koby snapped off the light and crawled into bed. Things seemed so wrong. She missed the gentle rocking, the escape hatch, the bow pulpit, the wind slapping halyards, and waves lapping against the hull.

Crying softly, Koby lay awake listening to strange noises she did not like—dogs barking, sirens, cars speeding past, funny-sounding footsteps, people's voices. And she smelled musky smells. She actually missed Mom and Dad's arguing. What was Dad doing right now alone onboard *Dream Chaser*? Koby's crying built into jerking, hiccuping sobs that came like waves crashing ashore.

Sleep refused to come. Hours later, still awake, Koby crawled from the bed and groped in the dark for her insert and leggy. She pulled them on without tightening the strap. Tossing and turning in a strange bed had made her body ache. Quietly she opened the door. Hand over hand she felt her way down the hallway to the next room. She opened the door and crossed over until she bumped into her mom's bed. Trying to be quiet, she pulled off her leggy and crawled under the covers.

"Koby, are you okay, honey?" Paige asked, startled.

Koby did not answer. She cuddled tightly to her mom's side and hugged. Paige hugged back and stroked her hair in silence. For now that was all that Koby wanted. She fell into a deep sleep filled with dreams of halyards clinking musically against a mast.

In the morning, Koby woke up confused. Where was she? As she rubbed crusted tears from her sore eyes, she remembered. Tess Morgan's. Loud, gabby Tess Morgan's. Dawn's gray light left dark shadows in the room. Koby glanced at her mom still asleep beside her. She felt embarrassed being here—she was a grown girl now. Silently she slipped from under the sheet.

Early morning held strange noises—cars driving by, a faint

droning sound, and a baby crying next door. There was an eerie feeling—as if the whole house had been welded to the ground. There should have been gentle rocking. There should have been the telltale lapping of water.

Koby balanced as she pulled on her insert and leggy. Tiptoeing with the leggy was like trying to drop a brick quietly. Before Koby could leave, Paige rolled over and opened her eyes.

"Koby, is something wrong?"

"I was trying not to wake you up, Mom."

"Oh, that's okay. What time is it?"

Koby shrugged. "It's getting light."

Paige sat up and rubbed her eyes. "Listen, honey. If Tess isn't up, maybe we can go for a little walk, okay?"

Koby nodded and returned to her room. She tried not to make noise as she changed. Everything looked out of place here. Her clothes should have been in the drawers under the V-berth and in the narrow hanging locker against the forward bulkhead.

Being quiet hadn't helped. By the time Koby finished dressing, Tess was up and visiting with Paige in the kitchen. So much for the quiet walk, Koby thought as she entered the kitchen.

"Look what dropped from heaven!" Tess exclaimed, greeting Koby with a big hug. "A hug a day keeps the blues away. Say, listen, how about if we plan something special after school. What do you think?"

Koby turned to her mom. "I have to go out and see the whales."

"Honey, don't you think they'll be okay for one day?"

Koby squinted. "Is that what you'd say if I was hurt?"

"Don't talk like that. When you were hurt, we took good care of you!"

"Now the whales need help," Koby said resolutely.

"This isn't all about whales, is it?"

Koby took a deep breath. "Mom, if I can't go out on the ocean, I don't want to live here."

"I didn't say you couldn't, it's just that . . ." Paige exchanged another one of her looks with Tess. "Honey, listen, Tess said you could keep the dinghy in the canal. After school, why don't you bring *Titmouse* here."

"After I finish looking for the whales."

Paige nodded reluctantly. "But I want you home for supper at seven, *understand*? And be careful!"

Koby nodded. "Aren't I always?"

"I won't answer that," Paige said, smiling.

"Well, now that that's settled, let's eat!" Tess said. "By the way, I think *Titmouse* is a silly name for a dinghy. Let's call it *Sunshine* or something." She ruffled Koby's hair.

Koby ducked her head and sat down at the table. "My dinghy's name is *Titmouse*!"

After breakfast, Koby caught the bus to school. All day thoughts of the whales obsessed her—it was as if she were in a daze. Finally the last bell rang and she hurried to the bus.

As she waited impatiently, she saw Becky Norman, Miss Perfect, walk from school. Laughing and talking with two boys, Becky tossed her long hair over her shoulder with a flick of her chin. What would it be like to have no problems? Koby wondered. To be a perfect person and lead a perfect life?

She tapped her leggy against the seat. Everything seemed in slow motion today. Finally the bus filled and pulled out, lumbering along at a snail's pace.

"Squid can run this fast," Koby mumbled to herself.

When at last they pulled into Pelican Harbor, Koby could hardly wait to get off. She wanted to take *Titmouse* out and open the throttle full—let the wind and salt spray blow away all her troubles. She headed for the dinghy, then remembered Nickeljack had wanted to see her first.

The old captain sat near the fish house playing out fish line, filing longline hooks. Squid rested some distance away. He'd found out that hooks could snag more than fish.

Nickeljack looked up as Koby approached. "Going out to the whales?" he asked.

"Yeah, you said to stop by."

"I know what I said. Here." He pulled out a bread bag partly filled with brown cream. The stuff looked like peanut butter. "This is for the cuts on the whale." He handed her the bag. "Now you remember something—that whale might not know you're helping her. Whales can slap you three shades of silly or ram you into whale heaven if they get scared. Understand?"

Koby nodded. She already knew from the lightning-quick bluff charge how Lady could attack.

"Remember, she knows a lot more about you than you do her. She can see right through you with her clicks and buzzes. That means she can tell if you're scared or angry. She knows if you're excited and if you're up to no good. Make sure to think the way you act. To be calm, think calm. Put the cream on gentle-like, okay?"

"Don't be such a worrywart," Koby said. "I'll be fine." Turning to leave, she looked back. "Aren't you going to tell me to take care of myself?"

"I just did, but you're not listening," he said.

"I'll take care of myself," Koby said. "I promise."

Nickeljack studied her, a troubled look in his eyes. "Good, 'cause this time *for sure* nobody else will!"

ELEVEN

Koby crawled into the dinghy and stuffed the plastic bag of cream into the side pocket next to the rescue kit. Could she find the whales again? she wondered.

First she stopped by *Dream Chaser* and changed into a swimsuit. She had hoped that Dad might be around. She wanted to hear his voice, hear him laugh, talk to him about her first night at Tess Morgan's.

But Dutch was gone, and so was the *Lazy Mae*. Disappointed, Koby angled out of the harbor. Once onto open water, she gunned the throttle and the dinghy leaped forward. She planed along in a daze, hair whipping at her neck and warm air buffeting her cheeks. Colter's Cut seemed empty and lonely. She quit trying to think. Thinking hurt.

After reaching open ocean, the easy slapping of the waves and the drone of the engine numbed her brain. Her eyes grew heavy. Even with the wind in her face, her head nodded. She realized how little she had slept the night before. But nothing mattered now except finding the whales. She shook her head and concentrated on staying awake.

The horizon stretched like a thin thread separating the sky and the ocean. What would happen if someone cut that thread? Koby wondered. She imagined the ocean swirling upward around the clouds. She imagined all the whales and the dolphins gliding like birds, with her among them. Free!

Koby looked around. In a few hours the sun would melt into the water. The hot air would cool. That was the best time of day—if a person didn't have to go ashore to Tess Morgan's crummy house. Thoughts of Tess snapped Koby from her daydreaming, and she slowed. She had reached the Cumberland Banks. Now she had to think about the whales. What if they weren't here? Deliberately, she looked.

For nearly two hours she idled about, searching the waves. Nothing broke the endless washboard water. Finally, she gave up—the whales could be anywhere. Koby glanced at the sun. If she wanted, there was time to return to Tess's the long way—going completely around the west end of Lonesome Key and under Three-Mile Bridge. Except for the shallow sand flats, it was a wide-open run up the gulf side. Today Koby did not want to get back even a second before she had to. One last time she scanned the ocean. Seeing nothing, she headed out.

The bottom grew shallow beyond Cumberland Banks. Koby slowed. Often boats ran aground on the sand shoals. Tide was high now, but even so, a shifting sand formation could lurk just beneath the surface. She angled toward the western shoreline two miles away. Carefully she motored along, at times in water less than a foot deep.

A mile ahead, a clump of logs appeared to be snagged on a

shoal. Koby changed her course slightly. Floating stumps and deadfall were something to avoid. A bent prop meant a long row to shore. Koby kept a sharp eye on the debris as she continued.

Drawing nearer, she saw odd shapes perched atop two of the logs. She squinted harder. It did not look like birds. Something else was odd. The curved and dark logs floated high in the water. She held her course. Suddenly one log raised up and settled. Koby blinked hard, then gunned the throttle directly toward the objects. Soon she had closed the last quarter mile.

"Oh no!" she gasped, staring. Her grip on the throttle weakened, and the motor died with a sputter. It was Lady and Squirt. They lay beside each other, stranded, half submerged on a wide and shallow shoal. Beyond them lay a third pilot whale. This one rocked on its side, bloated and dead in its watery grave. Deep gouges in the sand showed how hard all three had struggled. A rotted smell hung in the air.

Koby trembled and swallowed to keep from getting sick. What appeared to be something sitting on logs was each whale's dorsal fin. Huge chunks of flesh were missing from the dead whale's belly and side—probably ripped away by sharks. Koby wrinkled her nose and turned her head away from the terrible stench.

Lady's and Squirt's ribs stuck out. The skin on their big rounded heads and on their backs was dry and cracked. A dozen seagulls sat on Squirt's back, pecking out chunks of flesh. The calf watched with dull eyes, letting out a weak squeal. A shallow puff misted from his blowhole.

Beside him, not five feet away, Lady struggled to keep upright. She was the one that had moved earlier. As Koby watched, Lady rolled sideways, and her blowhole submerged. With a mighty thrash, she flopped and gasped a breath. A gurgling rumble came from her insides.

How long the mother and calf had been here, Koby did not know. One thing was sure. They were nearly dead!

"Go on, get!" she shouted, waving her arms at the seagulls on Squirt's bleeding back.

The gulls burst upward and circled. Koby studied the shoreline. The whales needed help, and soon! Kilroy's Landing by Three-Mile Bridge had the closest telephone, ten minutes away. If there had been a boat nearby, they could have radioed for help.

"I'll be back," Koby called loudly. She felt guilty leaving. The seagulls started landing on Squirt again. As Koby reached to start the engine, Lady listed sideways. Her blowhole slipped beneath the waves. The big whale grunted and thrashed her tail weakly but could not clear her hole.

"C'mon," Koby whispered. "Try harder!"

Lady relaxed and gave up.

"No!" Koby hollered. Without removing her leggy, she leaped into the shallow water. The seagulls on Squirt's back exploded into flight. Koby waded forward. She wrapped the dinghy's bowline around her wrist as she grabbed Lady's dorsal fin and pushed up hard. It was like trying to roll a heavy barrel. Slowly the whale rocked upright.

"Now breathe!" Koby grunted, bracing the dead weight.

Frightened, she slapped Lady's side. "Breathe!" Thin layers of black skin sloughed off on her fingers. "Breathe!" she screamed. The small valve of skin sealing the blowhole puckered closed. Frustrated, Koby slapped the blowhole.

Lady thrashed to life with an explosive blow. Chunks of blood and mucus spewed out in the misty blast.

"Yuck!" Koby grimaced—it smelled like vomit. A long minute passed before the whale blew again with a heaving cough. More chunks spewed out, speckling Koby's arms and swimsuit with red and gray and white. Still holding the dorsal fin, she couldn't let go to wash off.

Lady fell into her stupor again. Deep scrapes crisscrossed her blistered body like gruesome ticktacktoe marks.

"Try," Koby pleaded, grunting to keep the massive body upright. "Try, so I can get help."

Life flickered dimly in the whale's liquid black eyes. Each heaving breath sounded final. Koby looked around, frustrated. Her stump hurt from standing. If only a boat would come by so she could call for help. Overhead, the seagulls squawked.

"Go on!" Koby yelled, splashing at them.

The seagulls veered away but circled. Finally they gave up and descended on the dead carcass fifty feet away.

The splashing had wet the whales' dried and cracked skin, but precious minutes were wasting away. Where were all the boats that usually cluttered the shoreline? Soon Mom would pace up and down the canal wall like a nervous animal in a zoo. In another hour she would come unglued—or lose her ballast, as Dad would say.

Paige would get on the two-way radio and call the *Lazy Mae*. But that wouldn't help much. Only a hurricane would get Dad excited. He'd tell Mom to relax.

The ebbing tide tugged at the dinghy. Reflections of the setting sun spilled across the waves like red paint. The thought of being out with the whales after dark filled Koby with a sobering fear.

Because Squirt was smaller, he rested upright more easily. His gurgly blows came nearly every minute, more often than Lady's. Koby doubted the whales could last the night. Even if they could, how could she?

Still bracing Lady with her back, Koby pulled *Titmouse* close and threw out the anchor. Now the dinghy could drift about. To retrieve *Titmouse*, all she had to do was reach underwater for the anchor line.

The tide kept ebbing. Soon Lady and Squirt would rest in barely a foot of water. Someone had to come soon. They had to! Koby's mouth grew dry, but she knew better than to drink salt water. She waited, leaning harder against Lady. Haunting thoughts came with the long shadows. Tears wet Koby's cheeks.

As she leaned, sobbing, her knee pressed behind Lady's flipper. She felt a heartbeat. The weak pulse stopped her crying. She wiped at her tears, but the salt water on her hand made her eyes sting.

A small boat appeared in the distance, motoring up from a lower key a mile from shore. Koby waved wildly, but the boat angled toward Three-Mile Bridge and disappeared into the gulf. Koby's lonely and abandoned feeling deepened. Even if someone did search for her, they would be looking between Colter's Cut and the reef. Not on the sand flats beyond Cumberland Banks.

The dinghy taunted Koby. If she jumped in *Titmouse*, she could bring help in twenty minutes. All she had to do was let go of the big dorsal fin in her hand. But she still felt Lady's faint heartbeat. It held her like handcuffs, spellbound and helpless.

"I guess we're all stranded," Koby said aloud. The thought made her shiver.

Now dusk left only a pale red glow to stain the horizon. Lights blinked on along the shore. A string of cars threaded their way across Three-Mile Bridge, looking like a parade of tiny fireflies. Two more boats passed by, miles away. Koby knew that staying any longer was foolish, but she could not let go. Squirt stared helplessly. Lady's faint heartbeat ticked like a weak and distant drum. To leave would be to let Lady and Squirt die. The ebbing water splashed lower, tugging.

As darkness settled in, Koby made up her mind. "I'm staying!" she announced. "No matter what!"

The dead whale rocked in the waves fifty feet away. Stench from its bloated, rotting body carried with the breeze and mixed with the foul-smelling blows. It made Koby sick to her stomach. Finally she threw up and felt a little better.

Darkness drove away the seagulls and the burning sun, but it brought a terrible and numbing fear. No sounds reached out from the distant shore. Nothing existed except the maddening lap of the waves, the stink, and a thin sliver of moon.

"Lady," Koby whispered, "I don't know why all this is happening. It's not fair." A tiny reflection of the moon danced like a spark in Lady's glassy eye. Koby wiped sloughed whale skin on her blue swimsuit. She could barely make out the dark stains as she kept talking. "No matter what I do, it seems wrong. That's how my whole life is," she mumbled.

The ebbing water inched lower, making the whale's thick body sag against Koby. She strained. If the big whale rolled sideways, the water would cover her blowhole for good.

Koby's stump burned. It felt as if she had been kneeling on a hard floor for hours. Also her missing foot had begun to hurt. The phantom pain often hurt worse than any real pain. She tried changing positions. Her arms had grown numb.

Being stranded on a sand shoal surrounded by ocean and darkness caused Koby to reflect. Her dad played cards and often said life was just one big poker game. People couldn't choose the cards they were dealt, but they could choose how to play them. Koby figured she had been dealt the worst hand of any girl alive. What would happen if nobody searched for her? Or if they did, how would they find her? No matter what Dad said, there was no good way to play these cards.

The dinghy bobbing at anchor reminded Koby of the cream Nickeljack had made. It wouldn't do Lady much good now. Still, Koby grabbed the anchor line and pulled the dinghy close. As she fumbled through the side pocket to find the cream, her hand bumped against the rescue kit.

A thought caused her to pause. Inside the kit was a chemical light. Why hadn't she thought of it earlier? It would glow dimly for a couple of hours after being bent and the chemicals shaken together. It wasn't much, but it was something. Excitedly she tucked the bag of cream under her arm and opened the rescue kit. There it was! The cigar-size plastic tube seemed tiny out here on this big ocean, but it was her only hope. She tucked the chemical light in her suit and opened the bag of sticky paste. *Titmouse* swung back to anchor.

The whale did not move as Koby smeared the cream around her gashed flipper. There was enough left over to wipe some on the smaller scrapes and cuts. Lady lay motionless. Squirt's dark form appeared dead except for his blows, which grew weaker. Koby rinsed her hands in the water. Whatever Nickeljack had mixed up, it smelled gross! Tonight, everything smelled bad.

Having found the light buoyed Koby's spirits. But during the next few hours a deep loneliness flooded through her very existence. Far out to sea several ships crossed the horizon. From this distance, they probably couldn't spot car headlights, much less a tiny survival light. Koby shifted all her weight to her good leg. She was growing weaker. How long before her strength simply ran out? Overhead, the sliver of moon crept across the sky. Never had a night lasted this long.

Then something slid against Koby's leg, and she screamed!

TWELVE

Koby kicked hard into something slimy, and it snagged her ankle. She screamed again. At the same time she grabbed. Her hand came up with a big clump of seaweed. She stared, dumbfounded, then laughed to keep from crying. Her heart raced out of control.

Until now, Koby had not thought about sharks. Could the dead whale have swum here with the wounds it had? No, she decided. That meant it had been attacked here on the sand flats, probably by blacktip or lemon sharks. Suddenly the lonely night grew fearsome. Every splash of the waves or slap of the dinghy made Koby flinch.

The whales took longer between blows. Koby reached over more often to tap Lady's blowhole. The whale reacted each time with a startled chuff. Squirt seemed forlorn. Once he let out a long haunting whistle. Koby knew how he felt. Bone weary, she dozed as she leaned against Lady.

It was during one of these standing dozes that she started awake to a faint buzz wavering with the breeze. When it continued, Koby looked around.

East toward Cumberland Banks, a flicker of green and then red light could be seen.

"Hey, over here!" Koby screamed. She stopped. They wouldn't hear dynamite from this distance. She riveted her eyes on the faint light moving back and forth, back and forth. They must be out searching. Or else they were lost! Koby pulled the chemical light from her suit and gripped it tightly. She waited.

The buzz became a drone, and the distant light grew brighter, carving a path in and out from shore. Then it stopped. A thin beam from a searchlight flickered about.

"They're looking for me," Koby whispered, holding her breath. "C'mon!"

Again the boat droned and kept crisscrossing the water, coming closer. Koby let out her breath with a burst nearly as big as a whale's blow. The suspense made her shiver.

She knew that soon the sand flats would force the searchers to turn back. Only a fool would come across the flats at night. Now was her only chance. Hands trembling, she bent the plastic glow light in half to activate it. She shook the tube sharply to mix the chemicals.

The tube barely glowed. Failure knotted at Koby's throat. The boat turned again, inching along. Slowly the tube's green incandescence grew brighter and brighter. Koby braced the whale with her hip and waved the light—could someone see such a faint glimmer? When her arm grew tired, she changed hands, bracing the whale with her other hip. She kept waving frantically.

The boat slowed, then idled to a stop. Now Koby shouted,

her voice pitched with fear. If the boat left, it was all over. She had grown numb and faint. Her muscles knotted tightly and burned. Even now she braced mostly with her left leg to stop the aching in her stump.

The motor revved again, and the boat turned about. It moved away in a straight line.

"No!" Koby screamed, choking on her tears and swinging the light wildly. Her words strangled in her throat. "No! No! Please! No!" She stopped and stared, not trusting her tired senses anymore. *Was* the boat moving away? She listened, watched. Her breath stopped in her chest. The high-pitched whine of the engine wavered, then sounded louder. Koby shook her head. She was going crazy from being in the water so long. Having let the light slip to her side, she jerked it back above her head and waved it again in a big arc.

The boat was coming *toward* her. It had slowed entering the sand flats, but it *was* coming toward her. She could see both the running lights now. She gasped and kept swinging the light in frenzied circles. Squirt thrashed his tail.

The boat changed course, then angled back. They must be dodging sandbars, Koby thought, holding her breath to listen. The slow approach made her dizzy with excitement. Now Lady blew hard and flopped.

"It's okay, girl. Help's coming." Koby tried to speak gently, but her teeth chattered like marbles rolling down stone steps. Her body trembled as if a big hand were shaking her. She could not catch her breath to shout. The boat was very near now.

A coarse voice shouted something in the dark. Koby tried but could not speak. She coughed. The dim shape of a speedboat materialized from the night. A bright spotlight beamed on and knifed across the waves. It found Koby and blinded her. She shielded her face.

"Hang on. We're coming!" shouted a man. "This is the United States Coast Guard."

Koby still could not find her voice.

The bright searchlight traced Lady's ghostly shape head to tail, then flashed onto Squirt. The boat slowed to a dead idle.

"What in blazes!" exclaimed the man. The beam blinded Koby again, then played across the waves, finding the dinghy and the dead whale. Again the man exclaimed, "What in blazes!"

"I . . . I need help," Koby coughed hoarsely.

"Guess you do!" he said. "Ain't this a needle in a haystack." The big red-and-white striped speedboat floated to within ten feet, close enough for Koby to see two uniformed men. "Are you Koby Easton?"

"You found me!" Koby sobbed.

"You're lucky we did," the man in the bow said, a bit gruffly. He jumped over into the shallow water and waded toward her. "Bill," he shouted back, "call for help! Tell them the girl's alive and we have two whales stranded."

"Three," Koby said. "But one's dead."

The man motioned. "Come here; you're safe now."

"I can't let go."

"Don't worry about the whale; let's get you warmed up. Bill, get her a blanket. Warn them on the radio to be careful coming across the sand flats."

Koby braced her body stubbornly. "She'll roll over and die if I let go."

"We won't let her die, young lady." The man splashed toward her. "You shouldn't be standing there—whales can be dangerous."

Lady and Squirt started thrashing their tails.

"Slow down, mister, you're scaring them!" Koby scolded, coughing. "Easy, Lady. Easy, Squirt. Easy," she chanted.

The whales calmed. The man slowed his movement. "How long you been out here?"

"I don't know—what time is it?"

"The sun will be up in another hour. Here, let's get you in the boat." He grabbed her arm.

Koby jerked free. "Only if you hold the whale. She needs help."

The tall man looked frustrated and squinted into the spotlight.

"Go ahead, Brent," called the pilot. "Hold the whale for her."

"Right here," Koby instructed. Forcefully she placed the man's hand against Lady's dorsal fin. "If she quits breathing, tap your hand on her blowhole."

Koby let go, and the man grunted to hold Lady upright. Clumsy with cold and weariness, Koby stumbled toward the boat. The pilot reached over and hoisted her in by the arms. She collapsed on the floor.

"Here," the man said, his strong arms helping her onto one of the seats. He wrapped a blanket around her shoulders. Glancing at her leggy, he shook his head.

"Bill," the man in the water shouted. "I'm not going to stand here in the middle of a darn ocean and hold a whale all night."

"Quit whining!" the pilot said. "The girl's already done it most of the night. We'll have help soon."

Lady blew hard.

"Ah, jeez, she stinks!" the man cried. "And she's getting gunk all over me."

Shivering, Koby smiled.

THIRTEEN

An edgy breeze pried at the dark ocean. After hearing Koby had been found, her parents rushed toward the sand flats in their dinghy. By the time they arrived, Koby had warmed some but felt dizzy and weak.

Paige hugged her frantically. "You're safe! You're safe!" she stammered. "You scared me!"

"I scared me, too," Koby mumbled.

Dutch hugged Koby next, his huge burly arms not letting go for a long while. When he did, Paige motioned toward the dinghy. "Let's get you home."

"No! Lady and Squirt still need help."

"We're worried about *you*, mate," Dutch said.

"I'm okay. Really!"

Her parents exchanged doubtful looks.

Koby winced as she moved her leggy. "We can't go yet."

"How 'bout if we stay till it's light?" Paige said.

"Until they're safe," Koby said stubbornly.

"Let's see what happens," Dutch answered.

By the time traces of dawn streaked the horizon, a dozen

boats surrounded the stranded whales. Men and women in brightly colored wet suits crowded the shallow water. They held the whales upright and splashed water over their dried and blistered backs.

"Who are all those guys?" Koby asked the Coast Guard pilot.

"Well, a few are Marine Sanctuary Patrol. That tall lady is Dr. Michaels, a marine veterinarian. Beside her, in the gray wet suit, is Max Grogan. He's a marine biologist. The rest are volunteers from the local stranding network. They call themselves the Pod Squad because groups of whales or dolphins are called pods."

Koby couldn't believe all the commotion. It was so weird after spending the night alone. The marine radio crackled with nonstop talk. Volunteers spoke loudly as they splashed water over the whales. Dr. Michaels worked her way around the whales, listening with a stethoscope. When she finished, she spoke intently with the biologist. Koby listened hard.

"She's too weak to be moved," Max said, pointing at Lady.

Dr. Michaels nodded. "A move would kill her."

Max shook his head. "Then I think she's suffered enough."

Koby ignored the raw pain in her stump as she vaulted overboard. "You're not going to kill Lady!" she screamed.

Paige rushed to the railing. "Koby, where are you going?"

Koby waded forward, grimacing with each step. "Don't you dare kill her!" she hollered. "You can't kill Lady!"

The group turned to stare.

"Who's that?" Max asked, turning. He studied Koby as she waded up. His crew-cut hair and stocky build made him look like a drill sergeant.

"She's the girl who found them," called the Coast Guard pilot.

"Listen," Dr. Michaels said softly to Koby, "this whale is suffering. A simple injection can end that."

"No!" Koby said. "If Lady wanted to die, she'd have done it last night."

"We need to end her suffering."

"No!" Koby shouted. "She's Squirt's mom!"

"Squirt? Lady?" Dr. Michaels puzzled. "Listen, I know how you feel. But we don't even know this is the calf's mother."

"It is," Koby said. "I helped Squirt be born."

"This calf wasn't born last night," Max said strongly.

"I know that. He was born two days ago inside Chissom Reef." Koby didn't feel like explaining, but she added, "I cut the mom loose from a shrimp net. Look at her right flipper if you don't believe me."

The Pod Squad volunteers whispered among themselves as Max bent to look at the gashed flipper.

Dr. Michaels reached under Lady's tail fluke and pressed on her mammary slit. White fluid misted out. "She's lactating, Max."

"If you kill her," Koby said, "Squirt will die. He needs his mom."

"She's right, Max," Dr. Michaels said. "If this is the calf's mother, we have to try to save her. The calf won't survive otherwise."

"I don't think there's a prayer of saving her," Max said.

"Is there any way to airlift her?"

Max stared hard at the whales and then looked over at Koby. She met his gaze with a hard and determined glare. Finally he bunched his lips and nodded. "It's a long shot." He turned to the Coast Guard boat. "Bill," he yelled, "try and get me a chopper with a sling for the mother. We'll take the calf by boat."

Wild-eyed, Lady started thrashing her tail. Koby pushed past Max and knelt in the water, placing her cheek alongside Lady's head. With her hands touching the whale lightly, she whispered, "Easy, girl, Squirt needs you. Don't die."

The large pilot whale relaxed; the look in her eyes softened. Weakly she whistled. The group hushed as Koby stood. Suddenly the water blurred and tilted. Koby felt herself falling.

A strong hand grabbed her arm. "You need rest," said a woman's voice.

Koby looked into the kindly face of Dr. Michaels. She blinked to clear the dizziness. As the world steadied, she turned to the silent group that watched. "Don't scare them!" she said. "Be gentle and quiet." Then painfully she let the tall veterinarian help her to the boat.

"That was good advice," whispered Dr. Michaels.

Dutch and Paige helped Koby aboard, a quiet respect in their eyes. Paige wrapped the blanket back around Koby's shoulders. "Honey," she said, "I'm so sorry I didn't believe you."

"It's okay."

"No, it's not okay. It might have gotten you killed. How were you able to stay out here all night?"

"They needed me."

Paige bent over and hugged her. "So do I," she whispered.

By the time a big red-and-white helicopter flew in low over the water, Squirt had been cradled in a sling and loaded aboard one of the boats. Koby could see people force-feeding the calf with a funnel and a tube. He lay still even with the chopper making a deafening *thrup, thrup, thrup*. Hovering directly over Lady, the helicopter lowered a long line. Sheets of salty spray kicked out over the waves as they rolled Lady into a large sling. Koby shielded her face.

The volunteers connected the line. Max gave a thumbs-up signal, and the helicopter thundered, lifting Lady out of the waves. Water showered down as she rose. Lady's short flippers poked down through holes in the blanketlike sling. Helpless, her great body swung lazily in midair.

"Where are they taking her?" Koby shouted above the deafening roar.

"We'll keep them right here on Lonesome Key," shouted the Coast Guard man. "Max has his boat basin netted off in a canal on gulfside."

Lady flopped weakly in the sling as the chopper headed away, carrying her low over the water. Koby imagined how terrifying it would be to come up from a life underwater and then to be flying! Did Lady know she was being helped? Koby wished there were some easier way.

"They won't hurt you," she whispered, wiping at her eye with the back of her fist. The chopper blast died away.

After both whales left, the boats disappeared quickly. The

Coast Guard men insisted on giving Koby and her parents a ride to Pelican Harbor. With both dinghies in tow, they worked their way out of the sand flats toward open water.

Gingerly, Koby pulled off her leggy and threw it in the bottom of the boat. She examined her raw and bleeding stump. Later it would have to be cleaned and treated. And later she would check on Lady and Squirt. Everything would have to be later. Now, exhaustion overcame her. Huddled in the seat, she nodded off into a deep, numbing sleep with no dreams.

The Coast Guard boat left the sand flats and growled loudly, heading northward. Koby did not hear it. She did not see the Coast Guard men eyeing her with admiration. Nor did she feel the cream her mom rubbed gently on her stump or feel the blanket her dad tucked more tightly around her shoulders.

FOURTEEN

As the sun climbed upward from the horizon, the Coast Guard boat droned northward. Koby's hard, numbing sleep insulated her from the world like a cocoon. The first thing she sensed was being lifted over the railing onto *Dream Chaser*. Powerful arms carried her down the companionway and forward into the V-berth. Hands tucked her in, stroked her hair, and someone kissed her forehead. Then she slept hard again. The easy rocking, the clinking of the halyards, the lapping of the waves became a blissful dream.

She awoke later to find her mom sitting on the bunk. Koby blinked hard and looked around the V-berth. Why were they back aboard *Dream Chaser*? And why was Mom here?

Paige saw her puzzling. "It's okay, darling. Your father thought you'd be more comfortable waking up here."

"Where is he?"

"Out working his traps."

Koby yawned and stretched at the sleepiness in her body. Slowly she sat up. "What time is it?"

"Noon. We already called the school."

Koby swung stiffly from the bunk. "I'm starved!"

"Bet you are. Listen, get cleaned up. I'll fix something to eat." Paige disappeared aft to the galley.

Koby rubbed her eyes. Bit by bit she remembered all that had happened. It seemed like a crazy dream, standing all night beside Lady and Squirt in a dark ocean. "Ouch!" she exclaimed, touching her chafed and swollen stump. The pain reminded her that the night had been no dream.

Carefully she undressed and hopped into the tight shower stall beside the V-berth. Normally Mom scolded her for using too much hot water. This morning, Koby turned the water on extra hot. Eyes closed, she tried to warm her chilling memories.

Paige knocked on the door. "There's clean clothes on your bed," she called.

Koby finished showering and dried off. Phantom pain from her missing foot hurt like the devil. She reached down and actually squeezed the air, trying to drive the sting away. It did not help. Koby gave up and reached for the clean sock laid out beside her stack of clothes. Gingerly she pulled it on and smoothed the wrinkles. Mom had already dried the insert and cleaned the leggy. Koby finished dressing and brushed the tangles from her hair.

In the galley, hot hash browns and eggs were served up. Koby sat and wolfed down the food.

"There's more if you want," Paige said, leaning against the companionway.

Koby mumbled a full-mouthed thanks. "Mom," she said,

swallowing. "You being on *Dream Chaser*, does that mean you and Dad are back together?"

Paige walked over and squeezed Koby's shoulder. Already Koby knew the answer.

"No," Paige said, "I just wanted to be here with you."

Koby stood from the table. "I'd better get to school."

"You don't have to go today if you don't want."

"I want to," Koby said. She didn't really, but she wanted even less to go back to Tess Morgan's.

Soon they boarded the dinghy and motored to shore. Paige crawled out and tied off. Koby followed, limping. As they headed for the parking lot, Koby saw Nickeljack cleaning fish beside the fish house. "Can I talk to Nickeljack a minute?" she asked.

"Sure, I'll join you."

"You will?"

Paige wiped her hands nervously on her shirt. "Honey, last night it was Nickeljack who told me you might be around the Cumberland Banks. He said he had a bad feeling."

"How did he know I'd gone there?"

"I haven't a clue, but I wasn't very nice to him."

"What did you say?"

"It's not as important as what I need to say now."

Silently they approached the old captain. He looked up, his hands bloody from cleaning fish.

"Hi!" Koby said. "Did you hear about the whales?"

"I reckon as everybody in Lonesome Key has heard 'bout them and you," Nickeljack mumbled, his face expressionless. "You all right?"

Koby bent down to pet Squid. "Yeah."

Nickeljack glanced guardedly at Paige.

Paige toyed with the ring on her finger. "Mister Nickeljack, I uh—"

"Mister makes me sound crooked," Nickeljack snapped.

"I need to say I'm sorry for yesterday."

The old captain raised an eyebrow. "Are you gonna?"

Paige nodded. "I'm sorry. I had no need to say what I did."

Nickeljack allowed a thin smile. "Okay, then let's pretend you didn't."

Koby had been nervously petting Squid. Now she stood and smiled. "Let's go see the whales, Nickeljack."

"They don't need me around."

"I called earlier," Paige said. "They're not letting anyone near the whales this morning. They said you could stop by later."

Koby nodded.

"See you, Nickeljack," Paige said.

"S'pose you will," the old man said, grabbing another fish from a big plastic garbage can filled with ice.

Koby waved good-bye as they left.

Seated in the station wagon, Paige looked over. "Is he always that way?"

Koby smiled. "No, he's not always that nice."

Paige shook her head as she drove. "I'll pick you up after school," she said. "We'll stop by the whales then."

Koby nodded. She was glad they hadn't left Lady and Squirt out on the sand flats to die. But it seemed wrong having them captive.

Before Koby climbed out at school, she leaned over and gave her mom a hug. "I'm worried about the whales," she said.

Paige returned a strong hug. "I'm just glad you're safe."

Koby watched her mom drive off, then limped into the brick building. Word had already spread about the whales. The secretary in the main office bombarded Koby with questions as she checked in. In the hallway, two girls stopped her.

"Hey," one said. "We heard you saved some whales."

"They're not saved yet!" Koby said guardedly.

The two girls acted nervous. "So," blurted the other girl. "Did you really stay with them all night?"

"Yeah." Before either could speak again, Koby walked away, trying not to limp.

Social studies class had already started when she walked in and handed Mrs. Larson her tardy slip. After she sat down, everybody kept turning to look at her. Koby watched the clock. In forty minutes, when the bell rang, she would not be able to avoid the flood of questions.

Slowly the class period ticked by, the clock on the wall marking each second like a time bomb. Five minutes before the dreaded bell, a knock sounded at the door. Mrs. Larson walked over. Outside stood a police officer. He whispered something to the teacher. She turned and looked directly at Koby. "Koby," she said loudly, "would you please go with Deputy Higgens."

FIFTEEN

Embarrassment warmed Koby's face as she limped toward the police officer. Why would they call her out of school? As she slipped out the door, away from her classmates' prying stares, the deputy nodded to her. "You sure must be important," he said.

"Why is that?" Koby asked.

"They need you to baby-sit."

"Baby-sit?"

The deputy started down the hall. "Those whales they brought in this morning, they're ramming the basin walls. Nobody can go near them. The vet, a Dr. Michaels, thought you might help."

"Me? Help?"

He continued, "Your mother will meet us there."

Tingling with excitement, Koby rushed to keep up with the man's long stride. Noticing her limp, the deputy slowed and asked, "Did you hurt your foot?"

"Yeah," Koby said, not wanting to explain. "I guess you could say that."

They crossed the parking lot and climbed into a patrol car. Soon they were driving fast across Lonesome Key. Koby glanced over. "Are the flashing lights on?"

The deputy looked down. "No, but maybe they should be." He twisted a knob on the dash.

"Did they need me real quick?"

"That was my impression."

"Would the siren get us there any quicker?"

The deputy allowed a thin smile. "Let's find out."

Koby's spine tingled as the siren wailed. She sat up and looked out. People on the sidewalks stopped to watch them pass. Koby waved. Angling down a back road to gulfside, she exchanged concerned smiles with the officer. She had no idea what she was supposed to do when they arrived, but she felt important.

She was still puzzling as they swung to a stop in front of a big white house. Cars lined both sides of the narrow street. Paige stood waiting beside their old station wagon.

Koby scrambled out as the deputy snapped off his siren. "Mom," she called. "Did you hear us coming?"

"All the way across town," Paige said, smiling as she crossed the drive. "I brought your swimsuit and some old clothes if you want them."

Anxious to see Lady and Squirt, Koby followed her mom around the side of the house. She found a boat basin the size of a swimming pool bordering the canal. Around the edges stood nearly a dozen people. Most wore swimsuits. At one corner of the basin a shallow ramp descended into the water. Plastic mesh fencing hung from red buoys, separating the basin from the canal. A sidewalk and neatly trimmed lawn surrounded the other three sides. Several tents were set up on the lawn.

Koby walked forward, trying not to limp. She spotted Lady and Squirt floating in the far corner. She also spotted the stocky man called Max. He still wore his gray wet suit. Closer to the pool stood Dr. Michaels, the woman who had helped Koby to the boat. She wore a T-shirt and baggy shorts. Most of the group turned to watch Koby approach.

Dr. Michaels smiled warmly. "Thank you for coming, Koby. Remember me? I'm Tracy Michaels."

Koby shook hands.

The man called Max walked over. "Hi, young lady. I'm Max Grogan. We might need your help."

"What can I do?" Koby asked.

"Since arriving, the mother has remained agitated. We can't feed, medicate, or take blood samples. She keeps ramming the walls and charging anyone who enters the water. We noticed how she calmed down when you talked to her out on the sand flats. It may not help now, but would you try?"

Koby walked to the concrete edge of the big pool-shaped basin. Overhead a baking sun shimmered down. Forty feet away, Lady floated beside Squirt, wild-eyed and chuffing. Several volunteers were cautiously approaching the whales from the far side.

"Here, Lady," Koby called.

The volunteers moved closer. Suddenly Lady slapped her tail and rushed toward them. Although weak, she crashed into the wall with a sickening thump. A rolling wall of water splashed over the edge. The men jumped back. Lady returned to Squirt with wheezing and coughing blows.

Frantically Koby screamed, "She's scared!"

Everybody stared in silence.

Dr. Michaels joined Koby beside the basin. "She's been doing that. I'm surprised she can even swim anymore. Soon she'll drown."

"Everybody's scaring her!"

Dr. Michaels backed up, motioning the volunteers to do the same. "I think she's protecting her calf."

Koby edged forward and lay on her stomach over the water. "Here, Lady. Come here."

Lady and Squirt remained near the net.

Koby kept calling and calling. Lady did not ram the wall, but neither did she come closer. She floated submerged except for her blowhole.

After ten minutes, Max called, "Koby, they're not going to come."

"Lady, can you hear me?" Koby pleaded, her voice tightening in desperation. She reached down and splashed the water. "It's me, Lady."

At the splash, Lady turned. She thrashed her tail and surged directly at Koby like a black torpedo. Without slowing or turning aside, she crashed into the basin wall. The dull thudding impact stunned her for a second, then she circled back beside Squirt.

Koby leaped to her feet in tears. "She didn't know me, Mom. She didn't even know me!"

Paige, Max, and Dr. Michaels walked forward.

"It was too much to hope for," Dr. Michaels said.

Koby stared hard at Lady. "If I could only get closer," she said. "If I could get in the water."

Max shook his head. "That's too dangerous."

Dr. Michaels nodded. "Max is right. She'd kill you."

"But she didn't kill me out on the ocean!"

"Maybe you were lucky," Paige said.

Koby sank sullenly to a sitting position on the walkway.

Max turned. "Tracy, that whale will kill herself if we don't free them."

"But she could never survive."

"Then we agree—either way she's dead!"

Koby looked to make sure no one was watching. Slowly she pulled her pant leg up and reached for the strap on her leggy. Holding her breath, she worked it loose.

Frustration showed in Dr. Michaels's voice. "So, that's *it*—we just let them die?"

Max motioned toward the ocean. "Out there they die with dignity. Not here in a canal basin with spectators."

"You call it dignity to die on a sand flat with seagulls and sharks pecking and chewing meat off your bones?"

"It's what's natural," Max insisted.

Koby let her breath out slowly. By prying with her thumb and pushing with her foot, she eased off her leggy. Then, fully clothed, she lowered herself into the basin. Cold water and fear grabbed at her breath.

Max was the first to spot her. He rushed over. "Get out!" he shouted, grabbing for her.

Koby pushed clear of his reach and sidestroked slowly toward the center, where Lady and Squirt floated.

"Koby," Paige shouted. "Get out! Do you hear me, *get out!*"

Dr. Michaels spoke more calmly, kneeling on the walkway. "Koby, if Lady doesn't recognize you, she'll kill you."

Koby kept paddling gently toward the center. Over her shoulder she whispered, "Then I hope she recognizes me!"

SIXTEEN

A hush settled over the boat basin as Koby continued toward the whales.

"Get back here this minute, *I mean it!*" Paige yelled, shattering the tense silence.

Koby glanced back but kept swimming—this wasn't schoolwork or dishes. No one else knew what had happened out on the ocean. No one else had helped Squirt be born or seen Lady's bluff charge. And no one else had stared all night into those haunting and liquid black eyes.

"Shhhhh," she said. "Not so loud; you'll scare Lady."

Red-faced, Paige stood, trembling. Dr. Michaels rested a hand on her arm. Koby kept sidestroking. Now the whales floated motionless only twenty feet away. They looked dead except for their grunting breaths.

"I'm behind you," Koby cooed. Deliberately she treaded water with her stump held forward—it was hard with her clothes on.

The calf squealed, and Lady flopped her tail to turn.

Koby recalled Nickeljack saying, "Whales can slap you three

shades of silly or ram you into whale heaven if they get scared." He had said, "Remember, the whale can see right through you with her clicks and buzzes. To be calm, think calm."

As Lady moved toward her, Koby conjured up warm thoughts of herself and Lady floating through the sky holding flipper and hand, whistling back and forth in whale talk. Soon only nervous ripples separated Koby from the whales.

Loud clicks and popping sounds from Lady's jaw shattered Koby's warm musing. Still she tried to relax. Friends had to trust each other, she told herself. Lady's clicks fizzled into a buzz as she glided within reach. Her eyes flickered. Squirt hung back, squealing and slapping his tail in alarm. Now Lady dipped her head downward. The sound of Koby's heart pounded in her ears as the last inches disappeared. Lady's buzzing tickled Koby's stump like a feather. This was how it had been out on the ocean.

"What's happening?" Dr. Michaels called.

"She's buzzing my stump."

"Then relax. She's sounding you with her sonar."

"I know." Dizzy with excitement, Koby forced herself to breathe more slowly. Finally the buzzing stopped, and Lady surfaced. Her wild glare had softened. She let out a long gentle whistle, like a sigh.

Exhausted from swimming in her clothes, Koby worked her way to Lady's left side. Lady did not move or startle. "You *do* remember me," Koby whispered. She grabbed the dorsal fin and eased against the large smooth body. Something nudged her back. She turned to find Squirt. All his cuts and scrapes made him look hideous.

"Oh, Squirt. How did all this happen?"

The volunteers had clustered around the walkway. Max stood shaking his head in disbelief. Dr. Michaels still held on to Paige's arm.

Koby called softly, "What should I do now?"

"We need them here by the ramp," Dr. Michaels said.

Holding Lady's dorsal fin and flipper, Koby kicked. Lady tensed. "Nobody's hurting you," Koby whispered. Once more Lady relaxed. Ever so slowly they drifted. Squirt floated beside them like a shadow.

"Keep working her this way," Dr. Michaels said, waving everyone but Max away from the ramp.

"What are you going to do to them?" Koby asked as her foot touched bottom. She eased the big animal in the last few feet. Squirt hung back.

"Take blood samples and blowhole cultures. They'll need feeding, too. Especially the calf." Dr. Michaels set a plastic medical kit at her feet. A stethoscope hung from her neck. She waded in slowly.

"You won't hurt them, will you?" Koby said.

"No, but we'll have to hold them, especially during feeding." She crouched and ran her stethoscope behind Lady's flipper, listening.

"Be careful," Koby warned. "Don't touch her cut flipper."

Dr. Michaels moved her hand. "You know this old girl pretty well, don't you?"

Koby nodded and smiled.

Dr. Michaels straightened. "She's in such rough shape."

"Will she be okay?"

"Can't tell yet." Dr. Michaels directed Pod Squad volunteers to move slowly along both sides of the whale. She pointed. "Koby, stand near Max, where Lady can see you and sonar you. Talk and let her know you're here."

Koby moved into position, glad that her pant leg hid her stump. "Mom," she called. "I need my leggy."

Paige brought the leggy, insert, and sock to the basin wall. She handed them down to a volunteer. The helper handled the leggy delicately, as if it had been freshly severed from a live person. Koby sat down in the shallow water. She pulled up her pant leg and fitted the sock and insert over her stump, then tugged on the plastic foot.

Everyone stole glances, pretending they weren't looking. Quickly Koby tightened the strap. Hadn't they seen somebody put on a shoe before? It really wasn't much different.

"Okay," said Dr. Michaels. "Everybody get a good grip. We'll draw blood first."

Two men held the tail fin and lifted. After having fought so hard, Lady now lay frighteningly still. Her ribs poked out like curved broomsticks under her skin. Her backbone protruded up nearly three inches. Dr. Michaels pulled out a syringe with a huge hypodermic needle. She drew bright red blood from under Lady's tail fluke. Moving forward, she used a large swab to scrape mucus from inside the blowhole. "Here, get these to the lab," she said, handing the culture and blood sample ashore.

"And somebody bring the gruel." She took a huge needle and gave Lady a shot behind her fin.

Max rolled up two towels. Prying the whale's jaws open at the corners, he forced in the towels. Koby wanted to stop him but held back. Volunteers pulled on the towels to force Lady's mouth open. Lady flopped weakly, then held still.

Dr. Michaels slipped a long plastic tube down the whale's throat. As Max held the attached funnel high, she poured a clear liquid from a plastic jug into the funnel. "This helps get fluids and minerals back into her," Dr. Michaels said to Koby.

Koby nodded weakly, nearly gagging. "What happened to the dead whale?" she asked.

"They towed it ashore and did a necropsy."

"A what?"

"It's like a human autopsy, to find the cause of death. I'm not sure what they found." Dr. Michaels kept pouring slowly.

"What will they do with the body when they're done?" Koby imagined a huge grave with a tombstone the size of a door.

"They'll tow it back out beyond the reef."

At last the clear liquid finished draining down the tube. Instead of removing the tube, Dr. Michaels motioned for a pail of gray, oatmeal-like mash. She saw Koby's puzzled grimace and smiled. "This is gruel. It's herring blended with antibiotics and vitamins. A lot healthier than a hamburger and fries." Slowly she poured the slimy gray mixture down the tube.

Squirt floated in front of Lady, making faint chirping sounds. Lady's eyes glistened, but she did not fight. She chuffed out a wheezy spray with each breath. After another quart of water was poured down the funnel, the long tube was pulled from the whale's throat. Dr. Michaels nodded, and the volunteers released the towels that held Lady's mouth open.

"Why so much water?" Koby asked. "Can't she drink salt water?"

Dr. Michaels shook her head. "In nature, all their fluids come from fish." She reached her hand over the blowhole and let an exploding breath cover her fingers with yellow slime and chunks. She studied it.

"What do you see?" Koby asked.

Dr. Michaels held out her spattered hand. "This yellow matter is mucus, but these hard chunks are tissue and blood. And these . . ." She pointed to several dark, stringy things. "These are roundworms. I'll have to treat them the next feeding." She pulled a tube of white salve from her pocket and rubbed it over Lady's cuts and scrapes. "This bad cut on her flipper is looking better."

"I treated it last night," Koby said.

Dr. Michaels raised a puzzled eyebrow. "With what?"

"Stuff Nickeljack gave me."

"Nickeljack?"

"He's a good friend of mine."

Dr. Michaels motioned for the group to release Lady. As they did, the mother whale rolled sideways. Everybody grabbed hold again to keep her upright.

"Okay," Max said. "Looks like we'll have to support her. Get three on each side. Start with one-hour shifts. Until the mother's stronger, we'll have to force-feed the calf."

Koby helped move Lady along the ramp as four more helpers surrounded Squirt and started forcing wrapped towels into his mouth. Squirt flopped back and forth, but the strong arms held him. Dr. Michaels and Max busied themselves again. They used a smaller tube to feed the calf a white, milky mixture.

Koby's leg ached all the way from her hip to the tips of her missing toes. Quietly she backed up and sat on the basin wall. The weight of her leggy made the pain worse.

Paige came up from behind and sat beside her. She drew a deep, deliberate breath. "Koby, that whale could have killed you!"

SEVENTEEN

Koby shifted positions to try and ease the pain in her stump. "Mom, I didn't have any choice," she said.

"Nobody made you disobey!" Paige said, her voice soft but firm.

Koby sat sullenly. Her mom didn't understand there had been no choice. Not here. Not on the ocean. When something was hurt, it needed help. Koby clunked her leggy against the basin wall. Sharp pain jolted up her leg.

"Quit that," Paige said.

Koby gave the wall an extra rap before stopping.

The sound of an engine droned up the canal. Koby turned and watched Dutch tie off. Her dad wore his work clothes and tall rubber boots.

"Hey, there's my little pirate!" he boomed, walking over with a lazy gait. "So this is where you've been hiding." His husky voice sounded forced. He exchanged nervous glances with Paige, then pointed at the two whales. "How are they?"

"Better, once they got help." Koby glanced accusingly at Paige.

Dr. Michaels and Max finished caring for the calf, then eased him into deeper water. Squirt flopped his tail and dived. Dr. Michaels walked up the ramp. "I'm Tracy Michaels. Are you Koby's father?"

Dutch shook her hand and nodded. "Dutch Easton."

"You have quite a daughter. You must be proud."

Dutch looked toward Paige. "We don't always show it."

Paige stiffened.

"So, how are the whales?" Dutch asked.

"It's been rough. That's something I wanted to ask you about. Lady needs everybody's help."

"What can we do?"

Dr. Michaels toyed with the stethoscope around her neck. "The whales may not live through the night. If they do, I'd like Koby here to help keep them calm. At least until Lady starts on solid food. That could take several days."

Paige bit at her lip. "She has school."

"The weekend's coming up," Dutch said. "I think our little mate could help."

Koby wanted to scream. Nobody ever asked her what she wanted. She spoke deliberately. "I want to help."

"If it's okay with the school, would that be okay with you two?" Dr. Michaels asked.

"Sure," Dutch said.

Paige nodded. "Why not—she's done everything else she pleases lately."

Dr. Michaels pointed. "She could stay in one of those tents or in Max's house. We have extra sleeping bags. Everyone's eating together."

"I'd love it!" Koby exclaimed. "Can I stay in a tent?"

Dr. Michaels nodded.

"I'll bring *Titmouse* over here," Dutch said.

"Dad," Koby asked. "Can you bring my fin and mask, too?"

"Sure. You plan on swimming with the whales?"

"She already has," Paige said wryly.

Dr. Michaels laughed. "Then it's settled. If you don't mind company, Koby, I'll join you in the tent. It's been years since I slept out."

Koby grinned. "Great!" She turned. "Thanks, Mom. Thanks, Dad."

"Be careful," Paige said.

"Well," Dutch said, "I'd best be getting back to *Dream Chaser*. You take care of my little pirate now."

"Dad, I'm not a little pirate anymore."

Dutch ruffled her hair and headed for his dinghy. He and Paige did not say good-bye.

Before Paige left, she gave Koby a smothering hug. "Here's your swimsuit and extra clothes. Call if you need anything else, okay. And *please* be careful."

"I will." Koby watched her mom leave. It felt good to be here, away from everybody she knew. She turned to Dr. Michaels and pointed to the outside shower beside the basin. "Can I use that shower?" she asked.

"Sure, that's what it's for." Dr. Michaels pointed. "You can change in that tent."

Holding her breath against the cold spray, Koby rinsed her stump and leggy. It felt good to get the salt off, but she hated cleaning her stump in front of strangers. The volunteers pretended not to notice, but she caught several stealing glances.

After toweling dry and dressing in the tent, she joined Dr. Michaels. Quietly they sat and watched the whales.

Lady still labored to breathe as volunteers balanced her upright. Max had propped up a hose so a fine mist drifted over the whales' dried backs. Several volunteers stood beside a picnic table discussing how to rig up a large sunshade.

"Will they be okay, Dr. Michaels?" Koby asked.

"Please call me Tracy," Dr. Michaels said.

Koby nodded. "Tracy, will they live?"

"Depends. Most parents will live or die for their young, especially mothers. I'm guessing that Lady will fight to live so she can care for Squirt. But if he dies, she'll probably give up."

"Some parents don't do much for their young."

"How so?"

Something inside Koby wanted to open up. She wanted to spill everything out where the late afternoon sun and the ocean breeze could get at it. But she didn't like talking about herself, especially to a stranger. "Everything I do is wrong!" she said.

Tracy squeezed her arm gently. "Seems to me that you've done a whole lot right. These whales owe you their lives. You're a brave girl."

"I was just scared," Koby said, picking at the concrete wall with her fingernail.

"When people are scared, that's when they sometimes do the bravest things."

Shouting on the front lawn made them turn. Two Pod Squad

volunteers crossed the lawn carrying boxed pizzas. "Donated compliments of Willy's Pizza Parlor!" one called. Everybody clapped.

"Chow's on," Tracy said. "Are you hungry?"

Koby scrambled to her feet. "Yeah!"

"Oh, Koby, I'd love to talk more later. And sometime I'd like to meet that Nickeljack friend of yours."

"Well, okay. Nickeljack doesn't like people much, but I think he'll like you."

As they walked, Koby eyed the tall veterinarian. Dr. Michaels wasn't like any doctor she had ever met. "Tracy," she said, "you're the first doctor I've ever liked."

Tracy turned and made a funny face. "Doctors are monsters: look out!"

Koby giggled.

Soon everyone gathered around the big picnic table and attacked the pizzas. Koby ate piece after piece.

Tracy called, "Koby, where are you putting it all?"

Without thinking, Koby shouted back, "I have a hollow leg."

An awkward hush spread through the group. Even the breeze seemed to pause. Koby wished she could chase after the words and stuff them back in her mouth. Embarrassment made her cheeks hot. She looked down.

Someone chuckled. This triggered snickers around the table. Tracy started laughing harder and harder, her mouth ballooning full with pizza. Finally she had to spit it out. That set everybody to howling.

Koby couldn't help smiling. She didn't like it when anybody laughed about her leggy, but this was different.

The rest of the meal, everyone talked openly to Koby, introducing themselves. Some glanced at her leggy, but most looked her in the face. Koby liked these people.

Later, one of the Pod Squad volunteers whistled loudly and shouted, "Hey, hey! Everybody listen up." He turned to Koby. "The Lonesome Key Pod Squad is making you an honorary member of our distinguished organization."

Everybody hooted and whistled and clapped.

"And in recognition of your brave actions, we present you with these." He held out a white cap and a T-shirt emblazoned with a colorful dolphin and the title "Lonesome Key Pod Squad Member."

Everybody clapped.

Koby couldn't believe it. She got shivers as she pulled the T-shirt on and adjusted the cap. Never before had she felt this important. She took a bow, grinning so hard she felt as if her ears were being pushed back.

That evening after feeding the whales, the volunteers held Lady in two-hour shifts. Dutch motored up the canal just before dark. He brought Koby's dinghy and equipment.

Beaming, Koby showed off her official T-shirt and cap. She told everything that had happened at supper.

"You'll become president on me if I don't watch out," Dutch said. He looked at his watch. "Well, I better be getting back."

Part of Koby wanted her dad to stay. Another part of her

wanted to be alone in this special world she had discovered. She watched Dutch start his engine and motor off into the gathering darkness. When the sound of his engine finally faded away, she crossed the lawn to her tent. Other tents crowded the lawn.

Tracy approached. "How's it going?"

"My parents need as much help as the whales."

Tracy raised an eyebrow but said nothing.

"Should I help hold the whales?" Koby asked.

"No, tonight you sleep. You did it all alone last night." She handed Koby a sweatshirt. "Here, it's getting chilly."

Koby didn't argue. The cool ocean breeze reminded her of the long night spent on the sand flats. It also reminded her of *Dream Chaser* and of all that had happened. She pulled the sweatshirt over her head. It fit like a tent, but she didn't mind.

Darkness had settled in, and the house lights were on. Sounds around the basin quieted. "I'm hitting the sack," Tracy said. She looked toward the basin with a troubled stare. "I hope they make it through the night."

"I'll be right back," Koby said, limping toward the basin's boat ramp. She rolled up her pant legs and waded in beside Lady and Squirt. The volunteers stepped aside as she leaned and touched Lady's side. She swept her hand under the big chin.

Lady's dull stare melted into the night.

"Don't give up," Koby whispered. "Your baby needs you."

EIGHTEEN

After toweling her legs dry, Koby crawled into the tent and found Tracy already stretched out.

"Did you say good night to the whales?" the veterinarian asked.

"Yeah." Koby zipped the mosquito screen closed. After undressing and pulling off her leggy, she squirmed into her sleeping bag. Her stump felt oven-hot from wearing the padded insert and leggy. Koby stared into the darkness. The whales' chuffing blows broke the stillness. Distant voices joined the sound of crickets.

"I'd forgotten how hard ground is," Tracy said.

Lost in thought, Koby grunted agreement. "Do you ever feel lonely?" she asked.

"Only when I don't have any friends. But today I found a new one."

Koby smiled. "Me, too." As she closed her eyes to sleep, she whispered, "Good night, Tracy."

"Good night, Koby. Sweet dreams."

Yawning, Koby said, "I'm going to dream the whales are okay and free again."

"That's a good dream. I can see them already, leaping across the waves like cloud shadow. Slivers of black dancing across an endless ocean."

"Chasing the wind," Koby whispered, drifting off.

Koby awoke with Tracy shaking her gently. "Wake up, it's time for breakfast."

Koby rubbed her eyes. "I'm not hungry."

"No, but the whales are."

Koby snapped awake and sat up. "How are they?"

"They made it through the night. We fed Squirt several times. He won't nurse with us holding his mother. Lady's heartbeat is stronger, but she still can't keep upright. You get dressed; I'll meet you down by the water, okay?"

Koby nodded. She squirmed into her swimsuit. The skin on her stump had rubbed so raw that traces of blood stained her sock. She grimaced and pulled on her leggy. If only she dared go without it.

The morning air was already hot and muggy. She crawled from the tent and limped toward the basin. Squirt floated a couple of yards out from his mother. Max mixed gruel. Six volunteers stood around Lady, wearing wet suits to ward off the water's chill. They waved good morning to Koby as she approached. She waved back.

Koby left her mask and fin on the ramp and waded into the cool water. This morning nobody seemed to notice her leggy. She dreaded another day, though, with the plastic foot pinching at her tender stump. Suddenly, on an angry impulse, she reached down and loosened the strap. She jerked the leggy off and flung it up on the lawn like a baseball bat. Several of the volunteers smiled.

Tracy laughed. "Remind me not to get you mad."

"It was hurting," Koby said with a quick smile. Never before had she exposed her stump in front of anyone except Mom and Dad. She took a deep breath and lowered herself into the water. The cool water felt like ice on her raw bulb of skin.

As Koby eased alongside Lady, the whale let out a weak whistle. Her eyes were dull, but her breathing sounded stronger. Squirt flopped and drifted closer.

"Danged if they don't recognize you," Max said, wading in with the feeding tube. "That's their first sound all night."

Gently Koby rested against Lady's chest, feeling each breath and heartbeat. She ran a hand over the cracked and flaky skin. Lady watched, blinking. This morning the mother whale did not struggle when her mouth was forced open. Slowly Max poured gruel into the funnel. Koby hummed softly.

"The cultures and blood results are back," Tracy said to Max. "Her white cell count is high, and she's fighting dehydration, lung worms, and a touch of pneumonia. I'll wait until she's stronger to treat the worms, but we'll keep giving her antibiotics."

Max nodded.

Tracy worked deftly, measuring medications, giving shots, applying salve, and drawing more blood. Koby knew all the treatment was necessary. She had been through it herself in the hospital.

"Koby, was the gash on the right flipper fresh when you treated it?" Tracy asked.

"Just one day old. Why?"

"It's healing amazingly well. What did your friend Nickeljack give you?"

"It looked like peanut butter but smelled really bad. We could ask him."

"I'd like that. Let's go after breakfast."

Next, they treated Squirt. The calf twisted and splashed as they held him for feeding.

"Is it okay if I play with him when you're done?" Koby asked.

"Sure," Max said. "But play gently so the mother knows it's play. By the way, what made you think Squirt was a male?"

"I don't know—he just seemed like one. Is he?"

Max gave her a puzzled nod.

To keep her mask from fogging, Koby spit on the inside. She kicked her fin and moved to deeper water to wait.

When Squirt was released, Koby kicked over into a shallow dive. The water was barely eight feet deep. She porpoised down and worked her way along the bottom. If only she didn't need air, how fun it would be to stay underwater forever. She circled and looked up, spotting Squirt's rounded belly. Near the ramp, six pairs of legs grouped around Lady's long underside. Koby let her breath escape slowly and eased upward.

When she touched the calf's soft underskin, he startled and twisted to look. Koby broke surface for a breath and dived again. This time Squirt watched her. At the last second he moved to avoid being touched. Koby wondered if maybe he was afraid.

Squirt splashed and came closer as if daring her, so Koby swam forward. Squirt slipped down and around. Lightning fast, he nudged her rump.

Koby surfaced, giggling. "He's playing tag with me."

Everybody turned to watch. Squirt glided forward, dodging and darting. Koby was ready for him and spun to face him. He flashed past, flopping his head in play.

Tracy called, "That's the best he's done since coming here. Make sure not to tire him, though. He's still weak."

Reluctantly Koby worked her way toward the ramp. Squirt kept nudging her and slapping his tail. Lady watched with a gentle glint in her eyes.

Koby waded ashore and pulled off her fin. She hopped quickly up the incline and picked up her leggy. Even though nobody seemed to notice, she couldn't get over the embarrassment when she exposed her stump. Quickly she rinsed under the basin shower.

"You'd give a kangaroo a run for its money," Tracy said as Koby finished.

"I beat Mom in a race once, me hopping on one foot."

"I can believe it. We should call you the human pogo stick."

Koby shouted, *"BOING! BOING! BOING!"* loudly as she hopped to the tent to towel dry. Tracy laughed. With a clean sock, Koby pushed into her leggy. Her stump felt better. Quickly she pulled on her blue jeans, tennis shoes, and her Pod Squad T-shirt and hat.

After finishing breakfast, they drove north toward Pelican Harbor. Koby stared out the window, smiling.

"What are you so happy about?" Tracy asked.

"I don't know. Maybe 'cause I'm getting to skip school and help the whales."

"That's a good reason."

Soon they pulled into the harbor. Koby spotted Nickeljack hunched over a waist-high wooden table near the boathouse. He worked, cleaning blue runners with a thin knife. Squid was curled up near his feet, waiting for boneless scraps to be thrown own. He always acted greatly inconvenienced whenever he had to stand to retrieve a piece. Charlie, the white heron, strutted warily along the wall, catching scraps of fish flipped his way.

"That's Nickeljack," Koby said, pointing. She crawled out excitedly. "That's him! And see his dog? That's Squid!"

The weathered old captain eyed them as they walked up. "I figured you'd forgotten where I lived," he said.

Koby presented her companion. "Nickeljack, this is my friend, Dr. Tracy Michaels."

With lazy eyes, Nickeljack looked Tracy up and down, inspecting the tall visitor as if she were a boat mast. His hands dripped with blood and slime from fish guts. With a wry smile and only a token wipe on his pants, he held out his hand to shake. "So you're one of them who had to pay for their learn- ing, huh?" he said dryly.

Tracy didn't hesitate. She reached and shook Nickeljack's gnarled hand, ignoring the blood and the fish guts. "The price of my education was a lot of money and hard work," she said, continuing to shake. "What was the price of yours?"

It was Nickeljack who finally pulled his hand away and studied the newcomer, curiosity shadowing his glare. "I ended up a bum, reckon that was my price." He spit on the ground. "Did you two come to flirt or are you lost?"

"We're here about the whales," Tracy said with an easy laugh. "Hope that doesn't disappoint you."

"I heard one died."

"He was dead when I found him," Koby said.

"Did you leave him be?"

"No," Tracy said. "We had him towed ashore for a necropsy."

"Then, I s'pose you'll sell all his teeth and bones to the tourists, huh?"

"His carcass has been towed back out beyond the reef."

Nickeljack flicked a chunk of fish gut off his pant leg. "That's what I want when I die. I want to be dumped out so the fish can nibble on me—give the ocean something back for all I took from her. I don't understand people the way they bury their dead in boxes so the world can't have nothin' back. It's selfish, don't you think?"

"Can't argue there," Tracy said.

Koby spoke excitedly. "We came to see what kind of stuff you made for Lady's cuts. Tracy says it worked good."

"That's 'cause it ain't witches' brew, like the stuff *doctors* use."

Koby wanted to kick Nickeljack in the shin and tell him to quit being so grumpy. She didn't dare.

"I'd appreciate finding out what the medication was," Tracy said, her voice businesslike.

"I s'pose you would."

"Nickeljack!" Koby exclaimed. "It's to help the whales!"

"Are you sure?" he said. "Sometimes old Ma Nature has ways of carin' for her own."

"The whales would be dead without our help," Tracy said.

"Sometimes being dead ain't the end of the world."

"What did you make for Lady?" Koby asked, impatience eating at her.

"Oh, don't get your feathers all mussed up. Come back this afternoon; I'll see what I can do."

"What's in the mixture?" Tracy asked.

"It depends. I mix whatever seems right—and that changes." He flopped another fish onto his short wooden board and started cutting. "Now some of us got work to do."

Tracy extended her hand. "It was a pleasure meeting you."

"I'll bet it was," Nickeljack said, not offering to shake.

Tracy waited patiently with her hand out. After several glances, Nickeljack grunted and gave her hand a slimy swipe.

Koby saw a smile tug at the veterinarian's mouth as they headed for the car. Nickeljack returned to cleaning fish as if he'd never been interrupted.

Out of earshot, Koby said, "Tracy, I'm sorry he was so grumpy."

"Oh no," Tracy said. "I found him absolutely engaging. We'll have to visit again."

"You did? I mean . . . well, sure, okay."

When they returned, the boat basin bristled with activity. Volunteers struggled with poles and mesh netting to make an umbrella of shade over the ramp area. A new shift of volunteers held Lady. Beside the picnic table, lunch was being cooked on a grill. A radio played softly.

Koby found herself thinking back to what Nickeljack had said, something about death not being the end of the world. Had he meant that it was better for Lady and Squirt to die? That couldn't have been what he meant.

Max met them on the lawn. "Koby, your mom talked to the school. If you miss less than a week, your only assignment will be to write a paper about all that's happened to you and the whales. Also, the school called and asked if your class could come on a field trip to see Lady and Squirt."

"My class? Here?"

Max nodded. "You don't mind, do you?"

"Uh, no, I guess not." Koby did not know how to explain that this new world was special and private, a world she did not want to share. Not with her parents. Not with her class.

The rest of that morning Koby hung around Lady and Squirt. With her leggy off, her stump felt better. She wore a sock when she wasn't in the water—the stump sunburned easily.

At noon Paige stopped by. She talked about Tess Morgan and told how last night they had worked in the garden and then walked down to the store before dark. Also she talked about starting work in the marina office and about Koby's school assignment.

Koby listened, bored and irritated. Not once did her mom mention *Dream Chaser* or Dad. After Paige left, Koby tried to relax and push everything from her mind. She could not. Her mind kept wandering back to the whales, to Nickeljack, and to her parents breaking up.

Later that afternoon, Tracy asked, "Koby, do you want

to go with me to get the medication from Nickeljack?"

"Sure, but aren't you scared of him? Everyone else is."

Tracy smiled. "Nickeljack isn't snapping at us. I've learned, at least with animals, that those who growl the loudest are usually scared or hurting."

"I don't think Nickeljack is scared of anyone. And he sure isn't hurt, at least not with a missing foot or anything."

As Tracy started to answer, a loud splashing erupted in the basin. Koby turned. Lady was flopping back and forth with chuffing spasms. The volunteers were struggling to keep her upright.

Tracy raced toward the ramp. Max ran over from the picnic table. Koby pulled the sock off her stump and took off hopping. In seconds she sat in the water, speaking softly beside Lady's head. She ran a hand gently under the big belly. Lady chuffed hard. Koby kept talking and rubbing. Slowly the whale blew shallower and quit struggling.

"Am I glad we have you around, Koby," Tracy said. "Let's let Lady settle down some, then try feeding her."

Max grunted agreement as the volunteers held the whale firmly. When Lady had calmed, Max brought over the tube, funnel, and a pail of gruel. "Everybody keep holding Lady. I'll feed her."

Awkwardly he tried to hold the funnel and pour at the same time. The funnel slipped.

Koby caught it and stood suddenly. "I can hold the funnel."

Max looked down at how she balanced with her stump visible and asked, "Are you sure?"

"Yes," Koby said, forcefully. "I'm not helping to hold Lady."

Max nodded. "Okay, grab my shoulder if you need."

Koby forced a sweet smile. "And you grab mine if you need." Carefully she raised the funnel and held it. She had learned to balance better on her single leg than some people could on two. Max snaked the tube in the side of Lady's mouth, pushing it several feet down her throat. Watching this made Koby swallow to keep from gagging. As Max poured the gray mixture, the funnel grew heavy. Koby strained to hold it high.

The gruel inched down the tube. Behind Koby, a commotion erupted. She looked back. Her whole class from school was pouring toward the basin. Already several kids stood on the walkway. Mrs. Larson, their teacher, was motioning for them to remain quiet.

Koby panicked—she was exposed! With her stump out of the water, she felt naked. Frantically she searched the lawn and spotted her leggy and sock. They might as well have been on Mars for all the good they were to her now. She dared not lower the funnel, and no matter how she positioned herself in the shallow water, her stump hung naked and visible. Now the whole class had grouped on the walkway surrounding the basin and was watching—even Becky Norman, Miss Perfect.

They stood quietly. Too quietly. Staring!

NINETEEN

With every eye in the class examining her, a sickening panic strangled Koby. Where could she hide? This was her worst nightmare.

"Should I hold the funnel?" Tracy asked.

Koby started to nod, then paused. Pride and fear tore at her. She had told Max she could hold the funnel. And she could! At the same time, dozens of eyes were piercing holes in her. It made her angry. This was her place, not theirs! The class had no right to be here. They hadn't saved these whales.

"Do you want me to take that?" Tracy asked louder.

Koby's mouth had become cracker-dry. "No!" she said. "I can hold it."

With a concerned smile, Tracy motioned everyone closer. Koby felt like a prisoner who had refused freedom. She watched the thick gruel creep down the tube.

Tracy whispered to Koby, "Have they ever seen you like this?"

"No, never!"

"Okay, will you trust me?"

"Trust you how?"

"Just trust me."

Koby nodded hesitantly. She kept holding the funnel up as Max tilted the pail farther. Gruel kept pouring out. Koby stole a glance sideways. Some students watched the whales. Most stared at her stump like a freak show.

"Okay, listen up, everyone," Tracy called. "Two nights ago, Koby Easton found this pilot whale and calf stranded out on the sand flats. Rather than let them drown, she held the mother upright throughout the night. She stayed out there alone, cold, and scared, until help arrived."

Tracy paused, studying each student. "Many of you think you know Koby Easton, but how much do you really know about her?" She pointed at Koby's bare stump. "We look down at a missing foot, and that's all most of us see . . . or don't see. These pilot whales see more. Much more! They look completely through you with their sonar. We call it echolocation. They know what you had for lunch, how excited or tired you are. They can tell if you're sick or well. And I believe they can tell if your intentions are good or bad. All this by echolocating your body.

"Koby is the only person these whales trust. With clicks and buzzes, they found something special inside her that might take you or me years to discover. They found a friend they could trust. This is a lesson we should all learn from these magnificent creatures. Somehow, to look inside other people." Tracy turned. "Thanks for letting me be your friend, Koby."

Koby felt herself nodding, but inside she felt something

much greater. Her classmates were still staring, but she didn't mind. They were staring at her now, not just at her stump.

As the gruel finished draining, Max poured a quart of water down the tube. Then he gently slid the tube from Lady's throat.

Arms shaking, Koby lowered the funnel. "Max," she whispered, "after you feed Squirt, can I play with him again?"

Max looked at the class of students. Smiling, he reached and took the funnel from her. "Go play first."

Koby remained standing. She pointed up at the lawn. "Can somebody bring me my fin and mask, please?"

Miss Perfect, Becky Norman, stepped forward and picked them up. She walked down to the water's edge and handed over the fin and mask, smiling, as if she were Koby's best friend.

"Thanks," Koby said plainly. She pulled on her equipment and swam out into the middle. Squirt did not offer to follow. Koby adjusted her mask and kicked over into a dive, angling up under Squirt. Before she could touch him, he pumped his tail and glided away.

Instead of chasing him, Koby turned and swam away as fast as she could. Squirt slapped his tail and dove after her. Alone in the middle of the basin, they began dodging, darting, splashing, and diving. Squirt raced in circles, trying to sneak up from behind. Finally Koby let him. Instantly a sharp nudge lifted her. Squirt surfaced and released a shrill burst of clicks and whistles.

The students broke into cheering. They watched as Koby cupped her hand and splashed Squirt. He reacted by circling and whacking his tail. Koby pretended to ignore him, floating quietly on her back. The calf bunted her several times. When

Koby did not react, he swam alongside, belly-up himself.

"He's copying you," Tracy called.

Koby smiled and ran her hand over Squirt's belly. He rolled upright and rubbed against her. Together they swam over and rested beside Lady's head.

The astonished students crowded about, asking questions. Soon Mrs. Larson called that it was time to go. Reluctantly everybody headed toward the bus. Over their shoulders they hollered thanks and waved good-bye.

"Thanks, Koby!" shouted Becky.

Koby hesitated, then waved back. She hopped over and sat on the grass as the bus started and drove away.

Tracy walked up. "Standing in front of your whole class took a lot of courage."

Koby toed a blade of grass. "It was stupid of me."

"Would it help if they could look inside you like the whales?"

"They would probably just see my guts and blood!"

Tracy smiled warmly. "When I was your age, nobody liked me because I was so tall. At least that's what I thought. I walked bent over and went barefoot, anything to make me look shorter."

"Being tall isn't bad."

"I know that now. One morning I woke up and realized I was the only one who didn't like me. Now I sometimes wear high-heeled shoes and big hats just for fun."

Koby sat a while, thoughts bumping through her head. "Being tall isn't the same as losing a foot," she said.

TWENTY

Returning to Pelican Harbor that afternoon, Tracy seemed eager to see Nickeljack. She strode ahead of Koby toward the seawall.

Nickeljack sat filing longline hooks. He watched them approach with a lazy stare. "Thought you forgot where the harbor was," he said.

Tracy smiled. "Not likely with you and Squid as landmarks."

Nickeljack frowned and kept filing.

"Has Dad been around?" Koby asked.

Nickeljack shook his head and jutted his chin toward *Dream Chaser*. "Just at night to sleep aboard his fancy bed."

"That's his dream," Koby said.

Nickeljack kept filing. "That boat ain't no dream. That's his dumb pride. You don't chase dreams with barnacles on your hull from not putting out." He lifted a hook level with his deep-set eyes and squinted. "This ought to catch something, don't you think?"

"Depends on who's fishing," Tracy said lightly. "We came to get the whale medication."

Nickeljack scowled. "I knew it wasn't for a prom date." He reached into his pocket and pulled out a plastic bag of brown paste. "Here."

Tracy took it. "Now, can you tell me what this is?"

"Just stuff I had handy, that's all."

Tracy squeezed the bag between her hands. "Should it be refrigerated?"

Nickeljack winked at Koby. "Wouldn't know, I don't have a refrigerator."

"Well, thanks for *all* the help."

Nickeljack spit on the ground and picked up another hook to file.

"Yeah, thanks," said Koby. She turned and followed Tracy back to the car. As they climbed in, she said, "Tracy, he acts mean but he really isn't."

"I know that." Tracy opened the bag of brown paste, smelled it, and wrinkled her nose. "I swear I need my head examined." She jerked the car into gear and spun the tires in the gravel.

"Nickeljack made you mad, didn't he?"

Tracy smiled. "Not that I'd admit."

Back at the basin, they smeared the brown paste on the whales' open sores. Lady and Squirt looked as if they had been in a peanut butter fight.

Max walked up. "What kind of medication is that?"

Tracy sneaked a smile at Koby. "I don't know the exact formulation."

"It's not peanut butter," Koby said.

"I should hope not," Max said. He waited a moment for a reply. When none was offered, he turned and walked off.

On the second day Squirt was fed every hour or two, Lady only in the morning and evening. By Friday, Lady could hold herself upright. Koby guided her gently around the basin. Still Squirt would not nurse.

Saturday evening, instead of feeding her gruel, Max slipped a whole herring in the side of Lady's mouth. He shoved the banana-size fish along her cheek into her throat. Lady thrashed her tail but swallowed.

"Why doesn't she want it?" Koby asked.

"In the ocean she wouldn't eat dead fish," Max said. "A dead fish would have something wrong with it."

After feeding, Lady swam slowly in circles. Max called everybody together to organize two-hour shore watches. Nearly finished, he announced, "Okay, we have the whole night covered except the graveyard shift. Anybody for getting up at two in the morning?"

Koby raised her hand. "I'll do it."

"Don't worry, we'll take care of it," Max said.

"Please?"

Max shook his head.

Tracy spoke up. "Anyone who can spend a whole night alone on the ocean saving these whales can surely sit on the grass and help watch them if she wants."

Max nodded reluctantly. He pointed toward a tanned volunteer standing near the picnic table. "Okay, you'll stand watch after Pete."

"Thanks," Koby said.

"You won't be thanking me at two in the morning. Do you want help?"

Koby smiled. "If I do, I'll wake up Tracy."

Tracy poked Koby in the ribs and whispered, "Like mud you will."

Koby giggled. "What if the wind blows the tent down or something? I'd have to get you up to save your life!"

"I'll make sure to set the stakes," Tracy said, winking. She glanced at the fading sunset. "You better get some sleep."

"Okay." Koby headed for the tent.

"Don't even think about pulling the tent stakes," Tracy hollered.

"I can already feel the wind coming," Koby called back, laughing.

After undressing, she lay down and listened to the muted talking by the basin. She felt happy—more happy than she had been in months, maybe years. If only she could ignore the questions that kept haunting her. What would happen if Mom and Dad stayed split up? How long would she have to stay at Tess's? And why hadn't Dad stopped by again? Koby made up her mind to take *Titmouse* and go see him the next evening. Maybe she could—

She never finished the thought. She fell instead into a deep sleep and did not hear Tracy come to bed.

It seemed only minutes after falling asleep that Koby blinked awake to a noise outside the tent. "Time for your shift," came a man's loud whisper.

Koby sat up in startled confusion.

"Are you awake?"

Koby rubbed at her eyes. "Yeah, I'll be right out."

"Okay," said the voice.

Tracy moaned and rolled over. "Is it two already?"

"Yup. Do you want to join me?"

She groaned. "I'm not even awake."

Koby stifled a laugh as she dressed. "It sure sounds windy out."

"I don't hear wind," Tracy grumbled, rolling over.

Koby finished pulling on her leggy, then unzipped the mosquito netting and crawled out. She moved quickly around the tent, pulling out stakes one by one. The whole while, she whistled and moaned like a dreadful wind. She worked until the ends of the tent collapsed inward.

"What's happening?" mumbled Tracy with a start.

Koby giggled as she ran toward the basin. Behind her she heard muffled grunts and tent cloth thrashing about.

Pete, the man who had awakened Koby, sat on the edge of the basin nearest the canal. Only ten feet away, Lady and Squirt floated motionless except for regular blows. A dim lightbulb beside the ramp cast an eerie yellow glow over the water.

"What's going on back there?" Pete asked.

Koby lowered her voice. "Somebody's tent stakes must have come loose."

Pete gave her an odd look. "Will you be all right here?"

Koby nodded. "Tracy is joining me soon."

"Okay, good night." Pete headed toward his tent.

Almost immediately, Tracy emerged into the glow of the yellow light. She worked at tucking in her shirt.

Koby fought back a smile. "Boy, that was a nasty wind!"

Tracy sat beside the basin. "A nasty ten-fingered wind. I should pretend you're a whale and stuff herring in your mouth."

"Are you mad?"

Tracy yawned a smile and shook her head. "Not a bit. Just figuring out how I'll get back at you."

For several minutes they sat listening to the music of the whales blowing. It sounded like old steam engines chuffing and whistling.

"Lady and Squirt act so much like dolphins," Koby said.

"They *are* dolphins."

"You said they were pilot whales."

"They're called pilot whales because their head is rounded like a whale. But they're really dolphins." Tracy paused. "When I first saw these two, I truly didn't think they would survive."

"Then why did you bring them here?"

She shrugged. "If they wanted to live, they deserved a chance."

"They wanted to—that's why they fought to stay alive out on the sand flats."

Tracy nodded. "They're making a remarkable recovery. Soon they'll be eating without help." She paused, toying with the cuff on her pants. "Koby, tomorrow I'll be returning to my work in Key West."

The words startled Koby. "But we just got to be friends," she said.

"And we'll still be friends. But life goes on."

"My life's come to a screeching stop!"

Tracy ignored the remark. "In a few weeks we should be able to release the whales. From now on, Max and the volunteers can handle things. You and I should get on with our lives."

"I don't want to go back to school. I want to stay here and help the whales."

"You've helped them all you can. What they need now is rest. I plan on stopping by whenever I can. You can, too."

"Could I come here and sleep?" Koby ventured. "I don't want to go back to Tess Morgan's—that's not home."

Tracy reached back and picked a blade of grass. Breaking off small bits, she tossed them into the calm water. "Sometimes life is hard to figure out. I do know we can't run from it. That gets us into trouble every time."

They sat silently for a long while before Koby said, "Tracy, why did Lady get stranded?"

"We may never know. She could have been sick. Maybe she stranded trying to escape danger. Maybe it was suicide."

"She wasn't trying to kill herself!"

"Why do you say that?"

"Because Lady loves Squirt; he's her baby."

Tracy nodded. "I tend to agree with you."

"What happens if they go free and get stranded again?"

"That's something that can't be helped. Life doesn't give guarantees. Koby, nobody can stay *here* forever. All of us, even the whales, have to go back out and face the world. This has only been a place to mend wounds."

"You can't mend a missing foot," Koby said sarcastically.

"Just make sure you don't run from it."

Koby chuckled. "Can you imagine being chased by a missing foot?"

"I'm not trying to be funny."

Koby pulled up her pant leg and tugged the leggy strap loose. She forced off the foot and waved it in the air. "It's coming to get you," she said in a devilish voice. "It's the missing foot of Lonesome Key."

"Quit it," Tracy ordered, laughing.

Koby held the leggy by the ankle and growled as she pushed it forward. "You better run."

Tracy squirmed back onto the grass.

Koby stood and hopped toward her. "It's coming to get you."

Tracy scrambled to her feet. "I don't believe this." She started running.

Koby hopped after her, shaking the leggy and growling. Faster and faster they ran, circling around the picnic table and past the tents. Tracy's giggling became hysterical. "Stop it or I'm going to wet my pants!" she gasped.

From a window in the house, Max yelled, "What's happening?" Several volunteers poked their heads from their tents and stared in stunned silence. "Is something wrong with the whales?" Max called again.

Tracy collapsed in a heap, and Koby landed on top of her with the leggy. Together they rolled on the grass, howling with laughter.

The yard light switched on, and Max sprinted across the lawn in his shorts. "What the devil is going on?" he said.

Tracy sat up smiling, holding the leggy. "I was just attacked by the missing foot of Lonesome Key!"

TWENTY-ONE

Max stared, dumbfounded. "What are you talking about, the missing foot of Lonesome Key?"

Tracy shoved the leggy at him and growled.

Koby giggled.

A reluctant smile played across Max's lips. He shook his head. "It's you two that need watching, not the whales." He stomped back toward the house.

Koby noticed all the gawking faces. "Let's see if the missing foot attacks tents," she said loudly.

Heads vanished, and zippers whipped closed. Koby smiled and tugged her leggy on. Still giggling, she and Tracy returned to the basin. They sat staring at the water.

"Tracy, I wish you were my mom," Koby said suddenly.

Tracy shook her head. "No you don't. You and I make great friends. But your mom loves you."

"She doesn't like anything I do."

Tracy bit at her lip. "Maybe she's afraid."

"Of what?"

"That you might get hurt again. It's hard to show love sometimes. Take me, I can hug a dog easier than a person."

"Me, too," Koby said. "Sometimes I wish I wasn't me."

"Everybody has problems," Tracy said. "Some people never open their bag of problems and they end up carrying them around. Others sort things out and wind up with barely a pock-etful."

"My bag fills up faster than I can dump it out."

Tracy smiled. "Seems that way sometimes."

"I don't think my pockets will ever hold all my problems."

"Not unless you do some serious sorting."

Koby sat quietly, thinking. Tracy made everything sound so simple. How could a person sort through missing feet, hurt whales, and split-up parents? "I feel like the world's biggest loser," she said.

A gentleness softened Tracy's voice. "The whales don't think you're a loser."

Koby leaned back on the grass. "Good, I'll let them work everything out."

"You'll figure things out. Just be patient."

Overhead, a million twinkling eyes looked down, reflecting in the mirror-smooth water. Koby remembered how this same sky had watched her out on the sand flats. That night it hadn't cared if she lived or died.

Squirt splashed, twisting about under Lady's tail. The dim lighting showed his insistent bunting.

"Look!" Koby said, pointing. "He's nursing."

"Marvelous!" Tracy said. She shifted positions to watch. "I've never seen a recovery this fast. You should be proud."

Koby beamed. If she never did anything the rest of her life, she had saved two whales. "Lady and Squirt talk to me," she whispered.

Tracy nodded. "I know. And they talk *about* you, too. They're regular gossipers. Maybe it's good we don't understand. Can you imagine what it would be like to be warm-blooded and breathe air, but still live in a dark and cold world and be hunted by sharks? You'd be caught between two worlds."

"Tracy, why don't people think animals have feelings? I know they do."

"I agree. When a dolphin loses a baby, she grows sad. You see it in her eyes. Often she drags the dead calf around for weeks. I've seen dolphins toss seaweed to people, sharing it, wanting to play. They peer up at you with that wondrous, curious look. And why does such a powerful creature not harm a person? Whales and dolphins seldom fight back, even when they're chased and herded into bays to be shot or clubbed to death."

"People kill them like that?"

"As long as we've existed."

"How could anyone do that to Lady and Squirt?"

Tracy bit at her lip. "For some people it's how they make a living. For most it's just greed."

"But dolphins and whales are special!"

Tracy shook her head. "Special is in the eyes of the beholder." Her voice turned sad. "Sometimes I look at how innocent and trusting they are, and I feel ashamed being a human—as if I've betrayed them. Does that make sense?"

"Yeah," Koby said.

"Dolphins and whales are from a different world. They're citizens of a blue planet that we can only visit. Most of those who kill them couldn't even tell you what they eat. It's easier to kill what you don't understand."

"I think I understand them some."

"I know you do. And all your life will be better for what you did out on the sand flats." Tracy looked wistfully out toward the dark ocean. "We have to learn to share with other creatures and other generations. This planet is one big school bus that has many more loads to haul. Often people act as if they're the last passenger."

Tracy breathed deeply and blinked as if she had just awakened. "I'm carrying on like a preacher," she said, standing and yawning. "Squirt has finished nursing, and it's four o'clock. Let's wake the next shift."

Koby nodded. She stared a moment at the whales. Silently she wished them good night, and she wished them a happy life.

"Who's on the next watch?" Tracy asked.

"Mike, in the red tent."

"I'll wake him if you fix our wind damage."

"Okay." Koby grinned as she limped toward the tent. She stretched the ropes tight one by one and pushed the stakes back in. Finishing, she saw Tracy appear out of the darkness. "Hope we don't have any more wind," Koby whispered.

"We won't. Even if I have to sit on you," Tracy said, crawling in through the front flap.

Koby followed. After removing her leggy, she stretched out. "Thanks, Tracy, for talking."

"Oh, thank you, Koby. Sleep tight."

"Yeah, good night."

When Koby awoke in the morning, Tracy was already up. Quickly Koby squirmed into her swimsuit. As she pulled on her leggy, white gooey paste squeezed out all over her hands and sock. She smelled it. Toothpaste! "Yuck!" she cried, jerking the leggy back off. The toothpaste smeared onto the nylon floor and onto everything she touched.

Carefully she unzipped the tent and reached for her towel. It too had been smeared with toothpaste. Koby gave up and crawled out. Hopping, she carried the towel and her leggy down to the shower by the basin.

Max sat on the wall with several volunteers, sipping coffee. "Jeez, you smell like a toothbrush," he said, fighting a smile.

"Where is Tracy?" Koby demanded, turning on the fresh water to rinse her leggy.

"She left for Key West early and didn't want to wake you. But she said you should brush your teeth when you got up."

Koby tried to keep a straight face. "I would, but I can't find any toothpaste," she said.

The kidding continued as she rinsed off. All the volunteers had heard about the collapsed tent and about the attack of the missing foot. Koby enjoyed the friendly joking. Around these people she felt like more than just someone with a missing foot.

After spreading out her towel to dry, Koby swam with the whales. She had played with Squirt only a few minutes when

Lady submerged and glided forward. Koby felt the tickle in her stump from Lady's echolocating buzz. Then Lady surfaced. Chattering, she threw her head sideways, dived, and glided past. Again she surfaced and whistled.

"Did you see that?" Koby called. "Lady buzzed me, and now she's playing."

The volunteers watched as the whales dodged and darted in circles. With abandon, Koby splashed and dove after them. When the play slowed, she grabbed Lady's dorsal fin. The mother whale towed her gently in a big circle. Squirt broke the surface. With a clumsy leap, he arched through the air, completely over the top of Koby. He hit the water, and the volunteers clapped. Koby grinned. If only her parents had been here to see this.

That afternoon, Paige stopped by. Quickly the stories of the past evening and morning came out. Koby told how the ten-fingered wind had collapsed the tent and about the missing foot of Lonesome Key.

"Some night the missing foot will come back to get us," one of the volunteers said devilishly.

Another volunteer told of Tracy's revenge.

Paige grinned at Koby. "I swear I've raised a delinquent."

Max spoke up. "Life around here would be boring without her. She even has Lady playing."

"She did play, Mom!" Koby said excitedly. "And Squirt jumped all the way over me."

Paige hugged Koby's shoulders. "How did I ever end up with such a crazy and wonderful daughter?" She turned and looked. "By the way, where is Dr. Michaels?"

"Gone back to Key West," Max said.

"So, Koby, are you ready to come home now?"

"To *Dream Chaser*?"

"No, to Tess Morgan's."

Koby looked to Max for help.

Max avoided her eyes. "The whales still need several weeks of good nutrition before being released, but not constant care," he said. "We'd love to have you stop after school to play."

Koby felt panic. She didn't want to go back to Tess Morgan's. Or back to school. "Could I stay here just one more night?" she asked.

Max looked to Paige. "It's okay with me."

"Please, Mom?"

Paige nodded reluctantly. "Okay, but I'll be by in the morning to take you to school. Then I want you back at Tess's. You understand?"

Koby lowered her head as she nodded. She felt as if she were being sentenced in a courtroom. She could hear the judge's somber voice. "Koby Easton, you are hereby sentenced to serve the rest of your life at Tess Morgan's. Each day you must report to school. Do you understand?"

Koby didn't understand. Nor did she want to.

TWENTY-TWO

Koby's last day around the basin wasn't the same without Tracy. By late afternoon only two volunteers remained. Even Max had left to run errands. Koby sat by herself on the basin wall with the whales lolling at her feet. They toyed with a small chunk of seaweed. No longer did their ribs show. Their skin was becoming smooth and shiny.

When Max returned, Koby helped him feed Lady and Squirt. She poked antibiotic and vitamin pills deep into the gills of the herring so Lady would not need shots.

"Can I see if Lady will eat without help?" Koby asked.

Max hesitated. "Okay, but watch your fingers."

Koby splashed a small herring in front of Lady's mouth. Max and the two volunteers watched. At first Lady only stared. Then, gently, she opened her mouth, and Koby placed the fish on her pink tongue. She swallowed it. Koby grabbed another. One by one Lady ate the whole bucketful. After the last herring, she chattered loudly for more. Koby reached in and patted her tongue.

"You sure do trust her," Max said.

"She knows I won't hurt her." Koby pulled her hand clear. Lady tossed her head and swam out to join Squirt.

"Max, tonight I'm going to go see my Dad. I might be gone a little late."

Max nodded understandingly.

Late that afternoon, Koby jumped in *Titmouse* and headed for Pelican Harbor. It bothered her that Dad had not visited. Choppy waves slapped the hull as a warm southwesterly breeze blew up from Cuba. Although clear, the air had a heavy feel.

Because it was Sunday, dozens of boats dotted the water. Koby angled astern of a large cabin cruiser and jumped its wake. *Titmouse* landed with a wild splash. Koby wiped salt spray from her face. Laughing, she waved to the smiling couple on board the cruiser. She could fit all of life's problems into a real small pocket if it were just herself, the dinghy, and the ocean.

Dutch was not around when Koby arrived. She spotted Nickeljack perched out on the breakwater near the harbor entrance, his elbows on his knees. It struck Koby as being odd because Nickeljack never just sat around. She motored over and tied off to a big rock.

Nickeljack appeared not to notice, yet she knew he had. She picked her way among the rocks and sat next to him. He did not speak or turn his head. Quietly Koby waited.

Finally he muttered, "I've been thinking."

"About what?"

"About something that don't fit well into words."

"Can you try?"

Nickeljack's cheeks twitched, and he bit at his lips as if something terrible were eating at his insides. Finally he coughed and started in.

"Once, when I was ten, I found a hurt cat—must have been hit by a car. Anyway, it was twisting and flopping and screaming something horrible, with blood coming out of its mouth. An old man stopped—he seemed old to me then. He picked up a stick and went to knock the cat on the head. I ran at him, kicking and shouting. I wasn't going to let him do such a cruel thing. I told him the cat was mine and that he couldn't hurt it. I remember him looking real sad. He dropped the stick and walked away.

"For another half hour I watched that cat flop to hell and back, me crying and shouting, 'You're okay! You're okay!' But the cat wasn't okay. When it finally died, it had suffered enough to give me a lifetime of nightmares."

Nickeljack swallowed several times before continuing. "I was only ten then. Now, supposedly, I'm grown-up. I've seen dozens of injured turtles, birds, dolphins, whales, you name it. But I've never forgotten that cat. That old man with the stick wanted to do the most loving thing he could. I didn't understand it then. I do now."

When Nickeljack had not spoken for a full minute, Koby asked, "Is it the whales that made you think of that?"

"I reckon those whales should have been left alone."

"Nickeljack, they didn't die! We saved them," Koby said. "Squirt has started nursing, and Lady is eating without help. Soon they'll be ready for release."

"Don't kid yourself."

"What do you mean?"

"No matter what they say, they're saving the whales for one of those fancy aquariums on the mainland."

"No, Nickeljack! Tracy said Lady and Squirt will be released. I believe her."

"Good, 'cause if you're wrong, you saved the whales to make 'em prisoners. Being prisoners is worse than dying. That's what happened to the last ones that stranded."

"Tracy wouldn't do that. Is that why you didn't like her?"

"Who says I didn't like her?"

"You sure were growly."

"Oh, that was just so I could get to know her."

"Funny way to get to know someone," Koby said.

"Yeah, but it works. Did you come to see Dutch?"

Koby nodded.

"He's had the *Lazy Mae* out a lot."

"Nickeljack, if you were my father . . ." Koby paused. "Would you get so busy you didn't come to see me?"

Nickeljack thought a moment, then shook his head. "I don't suspect I'd ever get that busy." He scratched his stubbled chin. "Nope, not ever."

Koby stood. "I'm going out to *Dream Chaser*."

"Dutch ain't been getting back till dark."

"Then I'll wait." She worked her way back across the rocks toward the dinghy.

"Take good care of yourself," Nickeljack called.

Koby turned and smiled. "I will."

Together they repeated, "'*Cause nobody else will!*"

Minutes later, she crawled aboard *Dream Chaser*. The sun had burned low into the water, a sinking shimmering ball of fire. Near the mast, Koby found a halyard down. From habit, she looped the line back up. Walking around *Dream Chaser* felt funny. When she lowered herself down the companionway, she tiptoed like an intruder. She called out, "Hey, Dad!" even though she knew Dutch was gone.

Dirty dishes were stacked in the galley sink, and clothes lay scattered about the salon. The cabin sole hadn't been swept for days. It's a good thing Mom isn't here, Koby thought. She kept the boat shipshape and would blow steam out both ears if she saw it now.

Koby wandered forward and stared at the V-berth. The empty cabin made her feel lonely. The rest of the boat looked like it had been rolled upside down—as if a stranger had been living aboard. Koby started cleaning. She swept the sole and ran water for dishes. Piece by piece she hung up her dad's clothes.

After straightening things up, Koby went topside. Dusk had set in. She settled herself onto the bow pulpit. Because Max knew where she had gone, she planned to wait for Dad. All night, if she had to.

Try as she might, Koby could not imagine life with her parents split up. What would become of them apart? Another thing bothered Koby. Could Nickeljack be right about the whales? He had never ever lied to her before. What if Lady and Squirt weren't released? She stared at the confused water lapping about the hull.

The hollow rumble of *Lazy Mae*'s diesel engine drifted in on the night air. Koby recognized the sound well, yet tonight it made her uneasy. She turned to look. In the dark she could see green and red running lights rounding the breakwater. She remained seated and waited for Dutch to dock *Lazy Mae* and board his dinghy.

A few minutes later, he motored out. Appearing from the darkness, he pulled alongside *Titmouse*. The engine stopped, and he yelled, "Hey, mate! You aboard?"

"I'm forward," Koby called.

Dutch grunted as he climbed over the stern. "What are you doing here?"

Koby didn't answer, nor did she move as she heard his heavy footsteps approach from behind.

"Does your mother know you're out here?"

"No," Koby said. "She thinks I'm at the boat basin. Why haven't you stopped to see me?"

"There's a good-size storm kicking up out to sea. I've been checking all the traps and getting things ready in case it decides to come ashore. Besides, I figured you'd be busy taking care of the whales and all."

"You could've stopped and said hi."

Dutch shifted heavily on his feet. "I thought I might be a bother."

Koby felt tears coming to her eyes. Blinking did not help. She crawled to her feet. "Dad, I missed you!"

Dutch pulled Koby into his arms. "Don't go getting all worked up now. I should have visited."

Koby clung to her dad's thick chest. He was strong and solid. She held to him tightly. For the moment she was safe, and he would protect her. But what would happen when he let go? Then what? Who could she believe? Who could she trust?

Koby kept hugging until Dutch relaxed his hold. "I'm hungry," he said. "Have you had supper yet?"

She shook her head. "I'm not hungry."

"Oh, let me rustle up something for my little pirate."

"Dad, I'm not hungry, I just wanted to talk to you."

He motioned. "Well, come aft and visit me while I fix me some vittles."

Koby followed him. By the time she climbed down the companionway, he had the refrigerator door open in the galley. "Want a cold sandwich?" he asked.

Koby gave up and nodded. Why didn't Dad listen? Why couldn't he just stop and talk to her?

"Looks like you picked up around here," he said.

Koby looked down. "Mom would blow a fuse if she saw this mess."

Dutch cleared his throat. "Probably would. Good thing she's not aboard, huh?"

"Mom should be here," Koby said. "It's where she belongs. With us."

"Well, I didn't chase her away. Leaving was her idea, and she's too bullheaded to say she's sorry."

Koby didn't answer. She didn't like talking bad about Mom.

Dutch set a bologna sandwich on the table. "Do you want a glass of water? We're out of milk and juice."

"Water's fine." She picked up the sandwich and took a bite. Her teeth bit into something metallic. Spitting out the bite, she opened her sandwich. Under the bologna was a piece of aluminum foil.

Dutch belly laughed. "Meat a little tough?"

Koby stood. "I better be going."

"Ah, don't be upset—you just got here."

"I got here two hours ago," Koby said.

Dutch pulled the foil off her sandwich. "Why don't you throw a blanket up in the V-berth and spend the night? Your mother won't miss you if she's not at the boat basin."

"Dad, I told her that's where I was staying. I'm not going to lie to her."

Dutch shrugged. "Whatever pleases you, mate. I'll come up and see you off."

"You don't have to," Koby said, climbing the steps. "It might be a bother."

Dutch followed. As she loosened the bowline, he reached and pulled *Titmouse* alongside. "How much longer will you be staying with the whales?"

"Just tonight. Tomorrow I go back to school."

"Well, don't forget where *Dream Chaser* is moored. She ain't movin'."

"I noticed," Koby mumbled.

"And what does that mean?"

"Oh, nothing." Koby shoved off into the dark.

TWENTY-THREE

Koby welcomed the stiff ocean breeze as she raced *Titmouse* across the dark waves. The wind didn't have an anchor; it went wherever it wanted. Koby held her head high. She wished she were the wind.

By the time she motored up the canal to Max's boat basin it had been dark for over an hour. Stars glinted overhead. The hot night air felt steamy. Max sat up watching the whales. He waved to her as she tied off.

"I didn't know if I should be getting worried about you or not," he said. "I thought maybe you'd found more whales."

"Dad didn't get home till late. How are Lady and Squirt?"

"Good. They spent two hours tossing a piece of seaweed back and forth. Every twenty minutes Squirt takes a break to nurse."

"Maybe they need a toy."

"Maybe." Max looked at his watch. "You better get some sleep. Your mom is coming by early."

Koby nodded. "I'll stop by after school, okay?"

"Sure, you stop by anytime you want. These whales still have a week or two of mending."

"Then what?" Koby asked, her voice guarded.

"Then they get out of this lousy basin."

"You'll release them?"

"Of course. Why do you ask?"

"Oh, just wondering." Koby headed for her tent. She crawled in and pulled off her leggy. She was bone tired, but the question stuck in her head. Who was telling the truth about the whales? Nickeljack? Or Max?

Paige stopped by early the next morning to take Koby to school. She brought a change of clothes. Koby showered in her swimsuit beside the basin, then crawled into the tent to dress. Before leaving, she led her mom down by the water. Lady and Squirt floated out near the canal.

"Hey, Mom, watch this." Lying on her stomach, Koby slapped the water back and forth. The whales submerged and circled the basin, surfacing beside her hand. Koby kept splashing lightly. Slowly Lady opened her huge mouth, exposing her shiny teeth. Koby reached in and gently patted her tongue. "Good Lady, good Lady," she cooed.

Lady moved her tongue forward and back, slowly letting her mouth close. When her teeth barely touched Koby's forearm, she stopped. Koby did not try to pull back. She turned and looked up at Paige. "Neat, huh?"

Fear clouded Paige's eyes. "What if she bites you?"

"Then I have a missing arm to go with my leg," Koby said, trying to keep from smiling. Seeing her mom's concern,

Koby laughed. "She won't bite me; she trusts me." She pulled gently, and Lady let go with a contented whistle.

Paige sighed with relief. "How do you expect me to quit worrying when you're sticking your hands in a whale's mouth?"

Koby smiled, wiping her hand on her T-shirt.

"Well, we better head for school."

They rode in silence. Koby wanted to tell her mom about visiting Dad on *Dream Chaser*, but what was there to say? It would only make Mom angry.

When they stopped in front of the school, Paige turned. "I'll pick you up this afternoon and we can go see the whales. If you want, you can take your dinghy back over to Tess's."

"How long are we staying there?" Koby asked.

"Until we find something better, honey."

Koby did not try to hide her anger. "There's plenty of room on *Dream Chaser*."

Paige looked frustrated. "I know things aren't the best with Tess. But she means well."

"Mom, she talks like a radio!"

Paige motioned. "Go on now, you'll be late for school. We'll discuss it later."

"We shouldn't have left *Dream Chaser*!" Koby called back. Quickly she crossed the lawn without turning. She heard the station wagon drive away. Ahead, students sat idly on the front steps. They waved. Koby hesitated, then waved back. Rachel and Cindy, two girls from her third period science class, came running up.

"Hey, Koby, that was neat how you swam with the whales!" Cindy exclaimed.

"Yeah, and how you helped feed them," Rachel said.

Koby smiled, embarrassed. She remembered these two in the circle of faces staring at her stump as she held the funnel in the air. "It was nothing," she mumbled, looking down.

"It was fantastic!"

"Yeah! They know you."

Koby nodded.

"Could we swim with them?" Cindy asked.

Koby shook her head. "No, but you *can* help."

"How?" The two held their breath excitedly.

"Lady and Squirt need a toy. Can you get everybody to chip in and buy a big ball?"

"Sure."

"Thanks," Koby said, excusing herself. Immediately more kids ran up with questions. Inside Koby a small part of her wanted to run, but a growing part of her enjoyed the attention.

In each class that day, the teacher spent a part of the period asking about the whales. Koby told how the whales needed a ball, and everyone promised to help.

During lunch the principal announced over the PA system that donations could be dropped off in the main office.

With all the attention, Koby dreaded PE class even more than usual. *Everybody* would be staring. She waited until the bell rang before entering the locker room. Immediately girls gathered around the bench in front of her locker. Koby dared not change into her gym clothes.

"Where exactly did you find the whales?"

"What were you doing out there?"

"Weren't you scared?"

"What if they hadn't found you?"

Everybody kept bombarding her with questions.

"I have to get changed," Koby blurted.

The door opened. "Is everybody ready?" shouted Mrs. Hurley, the teacher. She stomped into the locker room and sent the girls scrambling to change.

Soon everyone but Koby had filed from the locker room. As she snatched up her sweatpants, she noticed a pair of shorts hanging behind them. Mom had sent them along to school, insisting they would be more comfortable in hot weather. Koby had never worn them. No weather had ever been hot enough to make her show her leggy at school.

Today, something made Koby pause. Hesitantly, she reached for the cotton shorts and pulled them on. Before she could chicken out, she stood and walked down the hallway and out onto the playground.

The class had gathered in a circle around Mrs. Hurley. As Koby walked up, a couple of girls turned and noticed her exposed leggy. They smiled.

"Now listen up, class," shouted the teacher. She held up two gunnysacks. "We're trying something different today—we're having a sack race. Becky, you and Sandy pick teams. Becky, you're first."

Becky Norman looked about the group. "I'll take Jane," she yelled.

As they chose sides, Koby sat down. She was used to being picked last. With more than a dozen girls left, however, Becky pointed. "I'll take Koby."

Koby scrambled to her feet in numbed disbelief. Miss Perfect had picked her. And not last! As she walked past Becky, she whispered, "You'll be glad."

Doubt showed in Becky's eyes, but she nodded.

After sides were chosen, Mrs. Hurley shouted, "Okay, line up!"

As everyone jostled for position, Koby walked to the back of her line. At the front, two girls pulled sacks over their feet and crouched for the start.

"Okay, hop to the fence and back, then give the bag to the next person in line," yelled Mrs. Hurley. "Keep both feet in the bag. Any questions? Okay, ready, get set, go!"

The two front girls took off hopping as fast as they could. By the time they had reached the fence, each had fallen a dozen times. After hopping and tripping back, the girls passed their bags to the next in line. Quickly these girls took off. Becky's team was slightly behind. "Go! Go! Go!" they yelled.

One by one, everyone took a turn. Try as they might, Becky's team fell farther behind. Even Becky Norman herself lost ground to a thin girl named Louise. Finally, Lindy, the short girl in front of Koby, came stumbling and hopping back toward the finish line. She was hopelessly behind.

"Come on, Lindy! Come on!" shouted Koby.

The last person on the other team had already neared the far fence as Lindy approached. With only twenty feet left, Lindy looked back and gave up. She fell to the ground laughing. The other team began shouting, "We won! We won!"

"Get up!" Koby shouted. "We can win!"

Lindy sat up, startled. "But you haven't run yet."

"Hurry!" Koby screamed. "We can still win!"

Lindy crawled to her feet in disbelief. Everybody looked at Koby as if she were crazy. Laughing, Lindy hopped across the line and fell again.

Koby jerked the gunnysack off the laughing girl. Fumbling, she climbed in. The other team's last girl had reached the fence.

"No way can you catch her," Lindy said.

"You watch," Koby answered. She fixed her eyes on the distant fence and started hopping. By putting all her weight on her left leg, she lifted her leggy completely off the ground. A thousand times she had hopped when no one was watching. Now, she told herself, it was no different. It took a few jumps to settle into a long steady hop. Faster and faster she pushed herself.

There was shouting. The other girl had fallen but was up again. Koby ignored everything and concentrated, driving harder with each bounce. At the fence, she spun around. Her opponent was already halfway back, stumbling, but still going. "Faster, faster," Koby whispered to herself. Her teammates were yelling now. Catching up seemed impossible, but the yelling and screaming kept her going.

The other girl looked back and began to hop more frantically. Koby concentrated only on the finish line. Fifty feet left.

Forty. Then thirty. Still Koby trailed. She knew she could not catch up but kept pushing. Again the other girl looked back. As she did, she lost her balance. A broom's length from the finish line, she tumbled in a heap. Koby hopped past and let out a happy scream. She had won!

A mass of bodies engulfed Koby, everyone shouting and clapping. Koby closed her eyes and smiled. She raised her arms high.

The girl who had fallen sat sullenly on the ground. "I *should* have won!" she yelled.

"You're a Jell-O head!" Becky Norman shouted. "You *should* have a brain."

"Now, now!" called Mrs. Hurley. "None of that. Everyone run once around the field, then get changed for your next class."

As the class rounded the field, Koby ran hard. Her stump was sore, but she didn't mind.

Becky caught up, breathing hard. "So, what else can you do well?"

Koby smiled. "You'll have to find out."

Becky returned the smile and kept running alongside her.

Back in the locker room, Koby began changing into her jeans and T-shirt. Sweat glistened on her skin.

"Aren't you going to shower?" said Becky.

Koby shook her head.

"Why not?"

"Just because."

"It's because you don't want to take off your fake foot and hop in front of everyone, right?"

Koby nodded.

Before Koby could say anything, Becky jumped up on the bench and whistled loudly. "Hey, everyone!"

"Don't say anything!" Koby whispered, slapping Becky's foot. "Please!"

Becky grinned. "Trust me." Again she whistled, and everyone looked. "Koby doesn't want to go in the shower," she announced, "because she has to take off her fake foot and hop. So, today everyone has to be like her and hop."

A moment of silence erupted into rowdy laughs. "Yeah!" "Okay!" "Let's hop!" Everyone screamed. Soon the whole locker room bounced with girls hopping about on one leg. It looked as if someone had spilled a bag of huge jumping beans.

Koby watched the spectacle in utter disbelief. Were these girls making fun of her?

"C'mon," yelled Becky, motioning.

Koby wanted desperately to run. But she also wanted to be part of the fun. Hesitantly she removed her clothes and tugged off her leggy. She drew in a deep breath of courage. Her hands shook as she pulled off her stump sock and stood quickly to hop toward the shower. The other girls cheered and hopped alongside.

In the shower, everyone balanced awkwardly on one leg. They were all naked, but not as naked as Koby felt with her stump showing. Becky announced that if anyone let their other foot down, their showers would be turned on cold. Soon several had paid the price for losing their balance. Their shrill screams echoed in the tiled shower room. Koby couldn't help laughing.

Even while dressing, everyone kept hopping until Mrs. Hurley entered the locker room. She stopped and stared at the bouncing mayhem, her eyes wide. "For Pete's sake, what is going on?" she demanded.

Becky yelled, "We all have to hop like Koby today. It's the rule."

"If you could hop like Koby it would be okay. But you can't. Stop it, everyone! Someone's going to slip and get hurt."

Reluctantly everyone returned to their two-legged world and began dressing. Koby found herself mad at Mrs. Hurley for ending the magic.

As they dressed, Becky watched Koby.

"What are you looking at?" Koby said.

"How does your fake foot fit on?"

Before Koby could answer, several other girls crowded around. "Can we see, too?" they said. The circle tightened. More girls gathered to peer down.

Koby cringed, looking up at the circle of faces. Reluctantly she nodded.

"It's okay if you don't want to," Becky said.

"It's not that I don't want to. It's—it's just that I've never done it in front of people."

"It's okay," Becky said. "We're being nosy." She turned to leave.

Without thinking, Koby blurted, "I'll show you." Everybody

turned back intently. Fingers trembling, Koby slipped up her pant leg and lifted her knee. Even with her stump sock on, she felt her face flush hotly. "This is my stump," she said, moving it forward and back.

The girls stared uncomfortably.

"Sometimes it gets sore if I don't keep it clean or if my sock is wrinkled," Koby said. "What's really weird is that sometimes I can still feel an itch in my toes even though they're gone."

Several girls grimaced. "That's gross!" said one girl.

"Your face is gross, Wendy!" said Becky.

Koby lowered her stump. Carefully she pulled on her insert. She held up her artificial foot. "I call this my leggy."

"Jeez, that's neat," said Becky.

"A missing foot isn't neat," Koby said.

"I—I mean, it's neat how they make a foot that you can take off and on," Becky stammered.

An awkward hush made the room extra quiet. "Does it hurt?" one girl ventured.

Koby felt bad for having gotten cross. She lifted the leggy and pretended to bite it in the ankle. "No, it can't feel a thing."

As everyone laughed, the bell rang. The group scattered to finish dressing.

That afternoon, Koby felt like a different person—someone she liked.

Twenty minutes before the last bell, the principal announced on the PA system that there would be an immediate assembly in the gym. All the classes crowded down the halls with no idea what was happening. The teachers and principal ushered every-one into the bleachers and motioned for quiet. Then one of the office secretaries walked in carrying a huge red ball, as big as a garbage can.

Koby stared in disbelief as the principal walked to the podium. "Koby Easton, we have a little gift for you to deliver. Would you please come forward."

Not believing her eyes, Koby limped down in front of the whole assembly.

The principal cleared his throat and spoke in an important voice. "I understand you have some big friends who need a toy. Would you give them this gift from Lonesome Key Junior High?" He handed Koby the ball.

Because it was so large, Koby held the ball to one side. Even then it was hard to see. Her eyes were blurring.

TWENTY-FOUR

After school, Koby relaxed on the lawn, waiting for her mom. Becky Norman and three other girls from PE class joined her, and they sat in a circle shoving the big red ball to each other. Becky was suddenly acting like a big buddy. After a few minutes the school bus horns beeped, and everyone except Becky and Koby jumped up and ran.

"Is someone coming to get you?" Koby asked.

Becky pointed. "I live just down the road in Coral Reef Estates."

"Coral Reef Estates—that's one of those big fancy places on the ocean, isn't it?"

"I guess. Where do you live?"

Koby rubbed at the grass with her toe. "I'm staying with Mom at this lady's house up on the north end. I used to live on a sailboat."

"Jeez, a sailboat? That's neat."

"It was, I guess." Koby picked a tuft of grass and twisted at it. "Becky, can I ask you something?"

"Sure."

"How come you talked to me today?"

"I've talked to you before."

"Not much."

Becky shrugged. "You always act mad and stare at me."

"I stare because you're so pretty."

Becky blushed. "I'm not pretty."

"Are you crazy? You're Miss Perfect. You have gobs of friends. And you always wear makeup and neat clothes and jewelry and things. I'd kill for hair like yours. All the boys like you."

Becky shook her head. "Not all of them. Boys can be real mean." She paused a moment. "Why do you always act mad?"

" 'Cause I'm missing a foot—nobody talks to me."

Becky shook her head. "I've been in Lonesome Key for two years now. I didn't even know you were missing a foot until last summer."

"You didn't?"

"I just thought you were weird for wearing long pants all the time. I finally asked someone why you didn't wear shorts."

"I don't want everyone to know about my leggy."

"Well, you should talk more and you should wear short pants—your leggy doesn't look so bad."

"You still didn't say why you started talking to me today."

Becky shrugged. "When your doctor friend told how you saved those whales and how they trusted you, I figured you must be okay."

As Koby started to answer, her mom drove up. Koby jumped to her feet. "What are you doing right now?"

"Sitting here on the grass."

"Do you want to go see the whales get their ball?"

Becky scrambled up. "That would be great!"

Paige stepped from the station wagon. "Who's your friend?" she asked. "And what are you doing with that?" She pointed at the ball.

"This is Becky Norman. Can she help us give this ball to the whales?"

"Sure." Paige turned to Becky. "Is it okay with your parents?"

"They don't care."

"Okay." Paige opened the tailgate, and Koby stuffed the big ball in. Soon they were headed along gulfside toward the boat basin.

"Where in the world did you come up with that ball?" Paige asked.

"Everybody at school helped buy it."

"Those whales sure lucked out meeting you. How did your day go?"

Koby leaned back against the door, smiling. "Today I got to know Miss Perfect." She nudged Becky and giggled.

Becky returned the nudge. "I got to know Miss Grouch."

"Miss Perfect? Miss Grouch? Who are they?"

"Just these two people we met," Koby said. She and Becky struggled to keep from laughing.

"Koby, tell your mom the stuff you did today."

"I'm all ears," Paige said.

Koby told what had happened, including the gunnysack race and hopping one-legged in the shower.

Paige shook her head in disbelief. "I'm just glad you didn't kill yourself." Turning onto the boat basin road, she asked, "Have you girls heard about the storm?"

"Yeah, a little." Koby remembered Dutch's talk about a big storm.

"It's still out a long ways. But they say it might become a hurricane and come ashore by the end of the week."

"What will Dad do with the boats?"

Paige stopped in front of Max's house. "That's not our worry anymore."

Koby scowled at her mom as she jumped out. She pulled the red ball from the station wagon and carried it back to the basin. Becky and Paige followed.

Max met them near the canal. "Now, *that's* a toy!" he said.

Gently Koby rolled the ball down the boat ramp and floated it toward Squirt. At first both whales ignored the big sphere. Then Squirt turned and clicked a couple of times. Soon Lady swung around, her clicks lower and more crackly. Squirt coasted up and nudged the ball, pushing it in a circle.

"Look!" Koby said, as Squirt bunted the ball from underneath and lobbed it into the air.

"Didn't take him long to figure that out," Max said. "Now he can do something besides harass his mother."

"Maybe I need a ball for Koby," Paige said.

Koby poked her mom playfully, then crouched and splashed the water. When Lady glided over, Koby greeted the whale by rubbing her tongue.

"Doesn't that scare you?" Becky asked.

"No, she wants a missing arm to match her leg," Paige kidded.

Playfully Koby splashed Lady. "How are you, big girl?"

The mother whale chattered happily.

"Radio says the storm out over the Atlantic is still building and headed our way," Max said.

Paige motioned toward the whales. "What will you do with these two if it becomes a hurricane?"

"We don't know. Hopefully we won't have to find out."

Koby stood up and studied the sky. She couldn't see any sign of a storm, only a few wispy clouds to the east. "If the storm comes, you would let them go, wouldn't you?" she said.

Max hesitated. "I wish Lady were a little stronger." He looked toward the open water. "Out there nature isn't always kind."

"People aren't, either," Koby said.

Max gave her a curious glance.

They watched the whales until Lady began playing with the ball, too. Then Koby turned to Becky and whispered, "Want a ride home in my dinghy?"

Becky wiggled excitedly. "Sure!"

Koby turned. "Mom, is it okay if I take Becky home with *Titmouse*?"

Paige chuckled. "All right, if you promise not to save any more whales. Be home for supper, you hear? I'm starting to forget what you look like."

"I will. Oh, Mom, can I borrow ten dollars? *Titmouse* needs gas."

"Do you have that much in your savings?"

"*Yes, Mom,*" Koby groaned.

Paige dug ten dollars from her purse. After saying good-bye to the whales, Koby and Becky headed toward the canal.

"You mean you have to buy the gas for your boat?" Becky whispered.

"Every other tankful—that's the deal I have with Mom and Dad." Koby did not tell Becky this ten dollars was not for gas. She held *Titmouse* and let Becky climb aboard. Soon they were idling down the canal.

"Does this thing go any faster?" Becky asked.

"Yeah, but I don't want to hit any manatees—they hang around the canals."

"Those big walrus-looking things?"

"They call them sea cows," Koby said, "'cause they graze on underwater grass."

"Are they dangerous?"

Koby shook her head. "I've swum with them lots of times. They've even let me scratch their bellies and their necks. They like their scars itched."

"Scars?"

"Because they're so slow, a lot of boats hit them."

After reaching open ocean, Koby twisted the throttle hard. *Titmouse* nosed up and leaped ahead, scampering recklessly over the waves. Koby hollered, "Do you want to go over to Pelican Harbor and see our sailboat?"

"Sure—what fun!"

Twenty minutes later, Koby throttled down to enter Pelican

Harbor. As she pulled alongside *Dream Chaser*, she waved at Nickeljack near the boathouse.

"Who's that?" asked Becky.

"A friend of mine." Koby didn't want Becky to meet Nickeljack. Not yet.

Becky's eyes bulged as they climbed aboard the sailboat. "This would be neat to live on!"

"Not as nice as Coral Reef Estates."

"That place is boring."

Koby pointed proudly at the bow pulpit. "I sit out there and watch the waves. Everybody has favorite places—that's mine. What's yours?"

"I guess I like playing video games at the store. But that's not very special."

"It is, if you like it."

"I don't really; there's just nothing else to do."

Koby motioned Becky below. "Let me show you where my bedroom was."

Becky stared wide-eyed at the V-berth. "Your whole bedroom was this tiny place?"

"Yeah, that's why I liked the bow pulpit. See, I could climb up to the top deck through here." Koby pointed at the hatch.

Becky shook her head as they returned topside and crawled back into *Titmouse*. "Do you want me to drop you off in the marina at Coral Reef Estates?" Koby asked.

"I guess; it doesn't really matter. My parents won't be home till late."

For the fun of it, Koby took Becky home by going through Colter's Cut. In the middle of the winding maze of mangroves, Koby slowed. Even during the day, the cut had an eerie magical feel.

"This is another one of my favorite places," she said. "I like to be here at night."

"I'd never come here at night. It gives me the creeps."

"That's why I like it."

"You're crazy, Miss Grouch."

Koby smiled. "Some night I'll bring you here, Miss Perfect."

They laughed as Koby opened the throttle again and raced out onto open ocean. *Titmouse* bounced across the waves, and Becky gripped the bowline. She faced into the wind with a strange smile.

As they approached the fancy houses of Coral Reef Estates, Koby examined the empty beach. "Here," she said. "Crawl back here and run the engine. I've got an idea."

"I can't run a boat!"

"If I can wear shorts in gym class, you can run a boat. Just hold this and turn it if you want to go faster."

"What are you going to do?"

"I want to try something—you're going to freak!"

Hesitantly Becky steered *Titmouse* toward shore. Koby reached into the side pocket and pulled out a small wrench. Quickly she tugged off her leggy and stripped it of the sock and tennis shoe. Her leggy was actually two pieces held together by a bolt under the heel. Sometimes that bolt came loose and her foot turned on her. She kept a wrench handy just in case.

One time her foot came loose in the grocery store. Because she didn't have the wrench along, she walked to the car with her foot pointed sideways. People tripped on curbs and bumped into each other gawking.

Koby giggled as she loosened the bolt. With a twist she turned the foot completely backward on her leggy.

"What are you doing?" Becky asked.

"You'll see; keep steering into shore." Koby tightened the bolt, retied the tennis shoe, and pulled her leggy back on. Becky slowed as the water grew shallow. With the tide freshly out, the beach was clear of footprints. "Okay, stop," Koby said. She jumped out and gave the bow a push.

"Tell me what you're doing," Becky insisted. "Don't leave me here."

"Just idle that way." Koby pointed downshore. With her leggy facing backward, she walked from the water up onto the sand, leaving deep footprints. She followed the shoreline a ways before cutting back into the surf.

Becky motored in to pick her up. She stared at the opposing tracks and giggled. Koby jumped aboard and pushed out. "It's the monster from Lonesome Key," she growled. "Beach walkers will think they've lost their marbles."

Becky chomped her mouth. "They'll swallow their false teeth."

After straightening her leggy, Koby headed south toward the marina. When they reached the dock, Becky crawled reluctantly from the bow. "I haven't had this much fun—ever," she said.

"Sometime let's go swimming with the manatees or snorkel out on Chissom Reef. I'll introduce you to Frank. He's a big green eel that eats out of my hand."

"I'll watch!" Becky paused. "Hey, Koby. What are you doing tomorrow after school?"

"Going to see the whales, why?"

"Debbie's mom is taking some of us up to Miami to go roller-skating. Wanna go?"

Koby shook her head. "I can't be out that late."

"We're going early. We'll be back by dark."

Koby hesitated. "I've never roller-skated, I mean, with my leggy and all."

"So? You never saved whales before, either. If I can drive a boat, you can roller-skate. It's a breeze. C'mon."

"Okay," Koby said. "If it's okay with my mom."

"Great. I'll see you in school." Becky turned and ran.

Koby waited until Becky was out of sight, then climbed ashore and tied off. Quickly she entered the general store beside the dock. After picking out two heart-shaped boxes of chocolates, she looked through the card rack for two identical cards. Satisfied, she walked up to the counter.

The gray-haired checkout lady who greeted Koby moved in slow motion. "Early valentines?" she said in a croaky voice.

Koby nodded. "Yeah, early valentines."

The lady rang up the sale and put the cards and chocolate in a bag. "Hope you catch whoever you're after with these."

"Me, too," Koby said, waving good-bye. Soon she was back on *Titmouse* and headed north toward Pelican Harbor.

When she arrived, she made sure Dutch wasn't around. Then she boarded *Dream Chaser* carrying one of the boxes of chocolates and one of the cards. She set both in plain sight on the table in the main salon. One last time she glanced at the card. All it said was, "I'm sorry!"

Before leaving, she filled the dinghy with gas. Many times she had used gas from Dad's storage tank. Today she felt as if she were stealing. She would tell him later. For now, he couldn't know she'd been there. Quickly she jumped back on *Titmouse*. Instead of stopping by Max's to check on the whales, she headed out to look for the *Lazy Mae*. She just wanted to be around Dad.

Throttle wide open, she cruised through the cut to oceanside and searched the shore northward. She kept inside the reef. Some distance off, *Lazy Mae* came into view. Dad was checking traps near shore. He looked up and waved as Koby approached. He wore his usual flannel shirt, baggy pants, and tall rubber boots. His silver beard flashed in the sun.

"How's my mate?" he called out.

Koby waved and smiled. As mad as she had been at him last night, she still couldn't wait to see him. She stopped the motor and coasted in. "How you doing?"

"I've done better," he said, giving her a hand aboard.

"What's wrong?"

Dutch looked out at the water. "Last month I had me a boat, a family, and a decent take of bugs. And now!" He raised his arms in frustration. "Now I got the bank nibbling at my britches. You and Paige are gone. And the bugs are scarce as whale whiskers." He looked at the eastern sky. "To top the pudding, there's a storm coming. I swear, mate, sometimes life's got no humor. And if she does, I'm the joke!"

"Can I help?" Koby asked.

Dutch broke into a broad smile as if all his troubles had evaporated. "You already have. You and *Titmouse* are the grandest sight I've seen all day."

"Is the storm going to be really bad?"

Dutch wrinkled his brow. "Just heard on the radio it might grow to hurricane strength by tomorrow. Could hit land the end of the week.

"If it does, what will you do?"

"Run, if I have to."

"Run?"

"I'll try to save one of the boats."

"Which one?"

Dutch twisted his face in a sad smile. "That's the sixty-four dollar question, ain't it? If I lose this tub, I can't earn money to pay for anything. If I save her, there may be no *Dream Chaser* left to pay for." He laughed a husky laugh as if life had played a good joke on him. "I lose no matter what, mate."

TWENTY-FIVE

As *Lazy Mae* rose and fell with the swells, Koby sat listening to her dad. He talked until he seemed drained of words. Koby had come to tell him about PE class, about the whales, about Becky Norman, and a lot of other things. Now none of her adventures seemed important.

"Well, time to get back to hoisting bugs," Dutch said, as if a work bell had sounded in his mind.

"I should go, too," Koby said. Reluctantly she climbed into *Titmouse* and headed toward Tess Morgan's. She found herself feeling sorry for Dad. There had been a loneliness and a hurt in his eyes. Somehow she never thought of him as someone who got lonely or scared or hurt. It made her sad.

Koby was late for supper but did not hurry. She was only a mile north of Tess's and could think better when she went slow. She tucked the other card and box of chocolates in the side pocket for later, after dark.

When Koby arrived back, Paige and Tess were already eating. Paige looked up with a sharp glance.

"Go wash your hands and come join us," Tess called shrilly.

"Yes, Mrs. Morgan," Koby answered mechanically, hurrying over to the sink. Why did adults always figure hands were dirty? Swimming in the ocean kept her hands cleaner than a whistle.

"Why are you late?" Paige asked.

"Got talking to Dad."

"You didn't tell me you were going to see him."

"Was I supposed to?"

After an awkward silence, Tess said, "Well, Koby, let's hear all about your day."

"It was all right," Koby muttered. "Mom, can I go roller-skating with Becky and her friends tomorrow night in Miami?"

"Roller-skating?" Paige did not hide her surprise. "Won't that be dangerous with your leggy?"

"What's wrong, don't you think I can do it?"

Paige shook her head with a chuckle. "No, you usually do anything you set your mind to. But, honey, it's a school night."

"We'll be leaving early so we can get back before dark. Please, Mom? All the other girls are going."

"Who's taking you?"

"One of the girls' moms."

Paige set down her fork and frowned. "I don't know. You can't even make it home for supper on time."

"I'm sorry, Mom. Please?"

"Oh, all right. But be home before dark. Okay?"

"I promise."

"Oh, I would so like to be there to watch you," Tess bubbled.

"The car is full," Koby said.

Paige gave Koby a warning look.

After supper the three of them settled in the living room to see a movie. It had been a long time since Koby had watched TV. Tess talked nonstop in her high-pitched childish voice, as if everyone were five years old.

Finally Koby gave up trying to watch the show and stood. "I'm going out by the canal," she said.

"Don't fall in," Tess warbled.

Koby let the screen door slam. "And what if I did?" she mumbled. She hurried over to *Titmouse* and pulled the card and box of chocolates from under the seat. In the dark, she quietly skirted the house and placed the gift on the driver's seat of Paige's station wagon. Her hands grew clammy, as if she were committing a crime. It was no crime to want parents together, she told herself as she returned to the canal wall and sat down.

The warm night seemed to hold its breath. Koby swatted absentmindedly at the droning mosquitoes. She was glad she had on her leggy. Bites on her bare stump itched like fire. Out on *Dream Chaser* there had seldom been mosquitoes. Usually a breeze blew across the deck.

Gazing down into the glassy black water, Koby thought about Tracy and what the veterinarian had said about people and their bags of problems. At school today, much of Koby's bag had been emptied, but stopping by the *Lazy Mae* had filled it right back up.

"Koby," Paige called from the screen door. "It's time to go to bed."

Koby pretended not to hear.

Her mom called louder, "Koby, did you hear me?"

"Yes, Mom." Koby stood and shuffled slowly toward the house.

Passing through the living room, she mumbled good night. She went to her room and crawled into bed. Tonight her brain was numb from thinking.

Exhausted, she slept.

Morning came early with a loud knock on the door. "Up and at 'em!" Paige called.

Koby sat up and rubbed at her eyes. She paused a minute on the edge of the bed, then reached down and ran her fingers over her chipped and battered leggy. She had a decision to make.

In the mirror beside the bed was the reflection of a girl with a stump. Sometimes that girl seemed like a stranger to Koby. Today the stranger mumbled, "It's no big deal."

Koby hesitated.

Louder, the mirror girl said, *"It's no big deal!"*

Deliberately Koby pulled on her leggy and reached for a pair of blue shorts. Not pausing, she tugged them on and headed for the kitchen. She felt undressed with her leggy showing.

Paige and Tess sat visiting over coffee when Koby arrived. Paige spotted the shorts and smiled her understanding.

"Oh, don't you look comfortable," said Tess.

Koby nodded weakly. Tess would never dream how *uncomfortable* these shorts felt.

A dozen times while they ate, Koby fought the urge to race back to her room and pull on her jeans. She gulped down her breakfast and ran up the block to catch the school bus before she could change her mind.

When the bus pulled up, everybody on board stared in surprise. Koby sat down and pretended not to notice. Some of the smart alecks bent over to look under the seats at her leggy. Koby reached her hand down and waved to them. She smiled to herself when the kids suddenly sat upright.

At school the gawking continued. Whenever Koby turned, she caught someone staring—sometimes even teachers. It angered and embarrassed her. What a fool she had been. Why *hadn't* she worn her jeans? And why *had* she listened to Becky Norman? Almost in tears, she walked up to Becky in the hallway between classes. "Everyone is staring at me," she said bitterly.

Becky shrugged. "Everybody stared the first day I wore braces on my teeth."

"That's different," Koby protested.

"They'll get over it. They're just staring 'cause they've never seen you in shorts before." Becky smiled with an impish grin. "You're kind of cute!"

Koby poked out her tongue in frustration. She couldn't help but like Miss Perfect.

"Hey, are you going skating with us?" Becky asked.

Koby nodded.

"We'll pick you up at four o'clock."

"Okay," Koby said, and headed for class.

As each period passed, the leggy became less and less of an attraction. Becky had been right. By the last hour, Koby had almost forgotten she had on shorts, except that she felt a whole lot more comfortable in the heat. Her jeans always itched and made her sweat.

After school, Koby rushed back to Tess Morgan's to get ready to go roller-skating. Nothing seemed right for roller-skating except maybe a paper bag over her head. Finally, she pulled on a clean pair of cutoffs. The other girls would be wearing shorts, and in Miami nobody would recognize her anyway.

Because Tess was in the kitchen, Koby slipped out the side door. Paige was working in the garden. She turned and looked at Koby's shorts. "How were things at school?"

Koby shrugged and tried to sound casual. "The shorts were no big deal. Everybody stared until their eyes got tired. Becky Norman said kids just stare at what's new."

Paige smiled a tired smile. "I'm sure proud of you. I wish things could be different."

Koby didn't know what to say.

"Honey, would you know anything about a box left on the front seat of the car?"

"I've been at school all day," Koby said innocently. Then, unable to resist, she pushed her luck. "What kind of box?" she added.

Paige sighed. "Oh, nothing, just somebody's sad joke."

Koby turned away. A sad joke, she thought. When somebody said they were sorry, Mom called it a sad joke! A horn beeped on the street, and Koby was glad for the excuse to escape.

"Have a good time," Paige said. "And be careful!"

Koby broke into a run around the side of the house. Their whole family was a sad joke.

Out front, four girls jostled and giggled in a big car driven by a woman who looked about the same age as Paige. "Hi, Koby!" Becky yelled. Koby broke from her angry thoughts and waved. Suddenly her decision to wear shorts seemed dumb. As she crawled into the backseat, she could feel the other girls, Julie, Kate, and Debbie, all looking at her exposed leggy. Even Debbie's mom glanced back. Koby wanted to open the door and run.

"Koby," Becky said, "I told everybody about the whales and *Dream Chaser* and *Titmouse* and about putting your foot on backward to make tracks in the sand."

"Can you really turn your foot around?" Kate asked.

Debbie leaned over the front seat. "Show us, please!"

Koby didn't have the wrench along, but timidly she pulled off her tennis shoe to show where the bolt was. Becky made a gruesome face, pretending she had discovered monster tracks. They all laughed. Koby relaxed.

As they rode, Julie took out nail polish and worked on painting her toenails.

"Can I do mine?" Becky asked.

"Sure." Julie handed her the polish.

Soon Kate and Debbie had painted their toenails, too. Finishing, they handed the polish over to Koby. "Okay, your turn," they piped.

Giggling, Koby took off her tennis shoe and brushed the bright red polish on each toe. "There!" she said, finishing.

"Now your leggy," Becky said.

Koby felt hot with embarrassment. "No, not my leggy," she said. "It's not real."

"So?"

"Yeah!" squealed the girls. "It would look neat."

"No, it's not my real toenails," Koby protested weakly. "I feel funny."

"Okay," Becky said. "We just thought it would be fun."

Koby grew suddenly angry at herself. Why did she have to make such a big deal out of her leggy? She pulled off her other shoe. "Give me the polish." Hands shaking, she reached awkwardly around her knee and began painting the chipped-up plastic toes.

"Here, let me help," Becky offered.

Reluctantly, Koby rested her leggy over the front seat and gave Becky the polish. Becky ballooned her cheeks, concentrating on each toe as if it were a masterpiece.

"How come you didn't paint mine?" joked Kate.

"'Cause Koby's leggy doesn't stink," Becky said.

They all laughed, including Debbie's mom.

Finishing, Becky said, "Ta-da! Now let them dry."

Koby smiled at the sight of her chipped-up leggy with five cherry-red toenails. She felt ashamed for having made such a big deal of it. "Thanks," she said.

"Okay, anybody else have a leggy to paint?" Becky said.

Everyone giggled. As the girls kept talking, Koby looked at the five gleaming toenails on her leggy. Inside, feelings welled up she couldn't explain. She wanted to cry, and at the same time laugh and hug each girl for being her friend.

An hour and a half later they reached the roller rink in Miami. As Koby followed the other girls across the crowded parking lot, she felt panic building. Loud music, bright lights, and dozens of curious people greeted them as they filed into the lobby. Koby would have given a million dollars to have worn long jeans. No matter what she had said, her leggy *was* a big deal. Her foot was missing. Her whole foot! She couldn't ignore that—nobody else did! People would not meet her eyes, but they all stared at her leggy.

Blaring music from the loudspeakers made talking hard. Koby edged into a corner to put on her skates.

Soon Becky skated up. "Do you want help?" she asked.

"No, I don't think so," Koby said, as she finished tying her skates. Hesitantly she stood up and shoved off from the seats. So far, so good. Tensely she pushed with her leggy and coasted forward again.

Becky clapped. "You've already done better than me. The first time I stood up, I fell on my butt."

Koby giggled nervously. Holding her breath, she stared at the floor and worked her way around the outer edge. She wondered if people were watching. Cautiously she glanced up. When she did, she tripped and sprawled flat. She glanced around. Nobody seemed to have noticed. Embarrassed, she scrambled back to her feet and kept going.

Koby gradually felt more at ease. She found that she could make her leggy turn by moving her knee side to side. The motion felt awkward but it worked. Cautiously she skated faster, not watching the floor as much. People smiled, and several talked with her as she skated round and round. After a while, the only ones still watching her were an older couple who held hands all the time. Every time they passed, they stared.

Koby tried to ignore them, but soon even Becky noticed their gawking. "Those creeps," Becky said, skating up. "Do you want me to go say something to them? Or maybe accidentally on purpose bump into them?"

"No," Koby said. "It's okay."

"It isn't okay. It's rude! I'm going to say something," Becky exclaimed.

"No, wait!" Koby shouted over the blaring music. "I have an idea. Go get everyone."

Becky nodded and soon returned with the other girls.

"Get behind me and push," Koby said.

"Why, what are you going to do?" Julie asked.

"Just push me, I'll show you."

Curiously they pushed. Koby lifted her leggy and tried balancing on her single skate. It worked. "Okay, push me up behind Mr. and Mrs. Eyeballs," she said.

Giggling, the girls pushed harder. Soon they circled in behind the unsuspecting couple. The two skated along hand in hand.

"Closer, closer," Koby urged. "Okay, hold me steady." She reached down and loosened the strap on her leggy. Carefully she lifted her knee and tugged off the plastic foot. She concentrated as she set her leggy with its skate on the floor and rolled it along. Then with a gentle push, she glided it between Mr. and Mrs. Eyeballs.

Other skaters saw what was happening and started to laugh. Mr. and Mrs. Eyeballs skated along, oblivious, until suddenly the unattached foot glided magically between them and out in front.

The couple stiffened as if they had seen a ghost. Then the woman screamed and threw her arms up. The man tried to turn as the leggy veered into his path. Eyes bulging, he ran directly into the wall. Catcalls and laughter drowned out the music for a moment.

"Thanks for the push," Koby said sweetly, as the girls let go. She coasted after her leggy. Catching it, she popped it on and tightened the strap.

Mrs. Eyeballs realized what had happened and skated back to Mr. Eyeballs. He stood dusting off his pants. Angrily the couple skated from the rink.

Although feeling satisfaction, Koby wished that everyone hadn't laughed so hard. She knew how laughter could hurt.

TWENTY-SIX

The magic of the evening lingered into the next day. Koby decided to wear shorts again to school. This time hardly anyone seemed to notice her leggy. Everyone talked about her prank on Mr. and Mrs. Eyeballs. Also there was talk about the storm still building out over the Atlantic.

After school, Koby rushed back to Tess's to change so that she could go and see the whales.

"You be home for supper by seven," Paige called as Koby jumped into *Titmouse*.

"This isn't home," Koby answered. Starting the engine, she motored down the canal. Soon she was racing across open ocean. She would be back by seven, but Tess's house would never be home. Not ever!

When Koby arrived at the boat basin, she found Tracy there, stooped over, looking at the whales. Excitedly she hollered, "Tracy! Tracy!"

The veterinarian straightened and waved, a big smile on her tanned face. "How's my favorite Pod Squad member?" she called.

"Great! Where is everybody?"

Tracy laughed. "I'm it! I stopped by to check on our patients and got corralled into watching them for the evening."

"How are they?"

"Fine, but I'm worried about this hurricane that's coming."

"Is it a hurricane for sure?"

Tracy nodded. "The National Hurricane Center in Coral Gables just upgraded it a couple of hours ago. Hurricane Lia, they're calling it."

"Will it hurt the whales?"

"I don't know. If we let them go now, they may be too weak to make it on their own. If we keep them here, a tidal surge could kill them."

"Can't you wait and release them just if it looks bad?" Koby said.

"By then the water will be too rough to get them out deep where they stand the best chance." Tracy made a fist. "I hate trying to play God."

Koby fidgeted uneasily. "Tracy, Nickeljack said you're going to send Lady and Squirt to an aquarium. He said that's what you do with all stranded whales and dolphins."

Tracy spoke slowly, choosing her words. "Nickeljack is partly right. That is often done. The aquariums are part of our stranding network. Supposedly they rehabilitate stranded mammals for release, keeping only the wounded ones that would not survive without help. But with the cost of dolphins and whales running into the tens of thousands of dollars, the aquariums sometimes figure out other reasons to keep them. I don't like the practice, and it won't happen with these two. You have my word."

"I sure hope you're right," Koby said. "Hey, you want to see something neat?"

"Sure."

"Watch this." Koby called Lady over and rubbed her tongue.

Tracy shook her head in disbelief.

"You know what else?" Koby told about the day at school and about roller-skating.

Tracy laughed hard.

Then Koby told about the boxes of chocolates.

The tall veterinarian grew thoughtful. "You've been a busy girl. What happens if the chocolates don't work?"

Koby shrugged. "I had to try something."

Tracy nodded. "I guess doing something is the first step in emptying out any bag of problems. I'm just wondering, though, if parents aren't a little like the whales. Letting them be free to do as they wish may be how you show your love for them."

"I don't think parents are like whales," Koby said stubbornly. "Besides, how would you know?"

A sad smile tugged at Tracy's lips. "I wasn't always married to my animals."

Nervously, Koby changed subjects. "What have you been doing the last couple of days?"

"I've been working on a sick dolphin we named Tiny Dancer. He was found stranded near Key West. Also two big loggerhead turtles, Mutt and Jeff, were brought in. They'd been tangled in plastic six-pack rings that someone threw away."

"It must be neat to work with animals all the time."

Tracy nodded. "It would be if their injuries weren't so senseless. I get herons and hawks with gunshot wounds. Turtles, whales, dolphins caught in discarded nets. Manatees hit by reckless boaters. It never ends."

"A lot of things in life don't make sense," Koby said.

Tracy forced a frown. "But we just keep trying to sort it all out, don't we?"

Koby made the same frown and said, "We just keep trying."

They spent the late afternoon relaxing on the lawn, visiting. Finally Tracy said, "Hey, you want to help feed?"

"Okay, if we do it quick. I have to be home for supper."

"In a flash," Tracy said. "Flash is my name, speed is my game."

They giggled.

After feeding, Koby heard a loud whistle. She turned to find Squirt rocketing toward her from the center of the basin. Twenty feet from the wall, he threw his head high and surfed in on his belly and flippers. A rolling wave gushed forward. Chirping and whistling, the calf tossed his head and dived with a sharp slap of his tail. Like gray lightning, he flashed under the big red ball and bunted it toward Koby.

"Guess who wants to play?" Tracy said.

"What time is it?"

"Seven."

Koby moaned. "I was supposed to be home by now! Would you call Mom for me and tell her you need me?"

"I won't do that, but I will call her and tell her Squirt needs you."

"Great!" Koby yelled, running toward *Titmouse* to get her fin.

In no time she was in the water, swimming, spinning, splashing, and hitting the ball. Squirt couldn't decide what he wanted to do—nudge her in the rear or bunt the ball. So he did both. Finally, chuffing for breath, he coasted alongside as if wanting Koby to hold his small dorsal fin. The fin still flopped to one side. Koby ran her hand along his chest. He let out contented squeaks that sounded like two balloons rubbing together.

Tracy returned and sat on the wall, smiling. Lady rested in one corner, seeming to enjoy watching her calf's antics. Every few minutes she raised her head and whistled. When Squirt finally ran out of steam, Koby swam over to the big whale. "Lady," she said, "Squirt couldn't have a better mom than you."

Lady made a soft crying sound.

Koby rested her cheek against Lady's head, and for a while nothing else in the world mattered—not her parents, not a hurricane. Nothing could ruin this moment.

It was after eight o'clock when Koby left. "Tracy, when will you stop by again?" she called from the dinghy.

"Soon."

Koby waved and headed back. Around Squirt and Lady, life became magical. She felt like hugging the world. Why did the magic disappear around her parents? When she left the whales, Koby wanted to cry and hide and give up.

She wondered what would happen now with the hurricane. She had never been through a big one. Dad would need help. The whales would need help. But what could she do? Life seemed like a big jigsaw puzzle. After the hurricane, would there be enough pieces left to put anything back together?

TWENTY-SEVEN

The hurricane's first breath came as a restless breeze rattling the palm fronds and petting the grass. Koby sat on the canal wall behind Tess's, hugging her knees and watching the shaggy whitecaps building on the ocean. The air felt impatient.

School had been canceled. Hurricane Lia, with sustained winds of over one hundred miles per hour, worried the Hurricane Center in Coral Gables. If she held her northwesterly course, she would come ashore in the next thirty-six hours somewhere in the Florida Keys.

Highway One through Lonesome Key was already clogged with cars heading north. People were leaving their homes, getting out ahead of the storm. In a way, Koby envied them. At least they had homes to leave.

Earlier she and Paige had helped batten down everything Tess owned. Inside the house, they moved things up off the floor in case of flooding. Next they boarded over the windows. Now Mom and Tess had driven to the store for extra groceries and flashlight batteries.

Koby wanted desperately to check on Lady and Squirt. Paige

promised they could run over with the station wagon later. Koby hadn't dared ask to go see Dad.

When she heard the station wagon pulling into the drive, she jumped up and ran to help unload. Tess had bought enough supplies to last through three hurricanes.

After the bags of groceries were safely stashed, Koby cornered her mom. "Now can we go see Lady and Squirt?" she pleaded.

"We'll have to make it quick." Paige turned. "Tess, will you be all right for a bit?"

"Oh yes, don't worry about me."

To avoid heavy traffic, Paige drove the back streets. Everywhere they saw people loading cars, boarding over windows, bracing or tying down things in their yards. Even the air seemed busy.

At the basin Koby found Max and Tracy nose to nose discussing the whales.

"But the hurricane could veer either north or south," Tracy insisted loudly, her hands lifted high.

Max looked like he was chewing on his tongue. "Okay, let's keep them here. But if we start taking a direct hit, I'll pull the fence down. We can probably herd them out to the canal mouth, but after that the waves will be too rough for us to help them."

"Is there something I can do?" Koby interrupted.

"All anyone can do is wait," Max said.

"Mom, can I stay here?" Koby asked.

"I want you with me during the storm," Paige said.

"Your mom is right," Tracy said. "You should be with your family."

"We don't have a family anymore."

Paige looked hurt. "Oh, honey, you'll always have a family."

"Do you mean we can stop and check on Dad?"

Paige stood, biting at her lip. "Okay, but just for a minute."

Koby followed Paige to the station wagon, and they drove in silence. When they arrived at Pelican Harbor, the *Lazy Mae* was gone. Paige seemed relieved. Koby spotted Nickeljack. "I'll be right back," she said, jumping out. "I have to see Nickeljack."

"Is there anybody you don't have to see today?" Paige said, impatience edging her voice. "Make it quick."

Koby crossed the parking lot to the boathouse, where Nickeljack was hauling equipment inside. He waved to her as she ran up.

"Do you need help?" Koby asked.

Nickeljack smiled. "Nah, mostly I'm putting away junk that could use a good hurricane."

"Does Dad need help?"

"I wouldn't know. He was in the harbor earlier, doing like other folks—getting ready to run if this windy witch starts coming ashore." Nickeljack raised an eyebrow. "By the way, did they let the whales loose?"

"They're not strong enough yet. If the hurricane hits Lonesome Key, Max said he'd herd them out to the end of the canal."

"He'd be hangin' pigeons in front of a shotgun, the fool."

"Nickeljack, he's trying to help!"

"Maybe the whales don't need his help."

"How would you know?" Koby snapped. "You haven't even come to see them. A lot you care!"

The old captain glared as if he'd been slapped.

Koby doubled her fists. "You're the one who told me how to find them."

"Maybe that was a mistake."

"Nickeljack, you act as if everybody's hurting the whales. You've never even seen them!"

"Don't have to," said the old man, grinding his jaw.

Koby threw her hands up in frustration. "And where are you going for the storm?"

"I don't know. I don't much care! I'm like a rat. I'll find a hole somewhere. Hell, this blow could dump us all into Louisiana."

The station wagon horn beeped.

"I have to go," said Koby. "If you see Dad, tell him I'll help, okay?"

Nickeljack nodded.

Again the horn beeped, and Koby took off running. "I'll be back," she shouted.

As Koby climbed into the station wagon, Paige said, "You two planning a picnic?"

"I asked him if Dad needed any help."

"Your father doesn't need help."

Koby spoke quietly. "All of us need help!"

The rest of the afternoon, Koby kept to herself, trying to ignore Tess Morgan's constant chatter. With each weather update, Tess worked herself into more of a tizzy. Finally Koby telephoned the marine office in Pelican Harbor. She asked if Dutch was around.

"He's been in and out like everybody else," the man said. "Haven't seen him lately."

"Has he left yet?"

"I heard him talking to some other boat owners. It sounds like they're gonna wait till daybreak to decide where to head."

"This is Koby. If you see him, tell him I'm going with him."

"Sure will." The man grunted good-bye and hung up.

When Koby turned, Paige was standing in the door. "You're not going out in a hurricane on any boat," Paige said firmly. The muscles in her cheeks twitched.

"But Dad is running away from the storm."

"That's not all he's running from."

"It'll be safe." Koby took a deep breath. "Mom, I'm going. If you needed help, I'd help you no matter what."

Paige walked forward and hugged Koby. As she did, she burst into tears. "I'm so afraid of losing you—you're all I have now," she said. "Please don't go out in the hurricane. I want you with me."

Koby squirmed free of Paige's arms and ran toward her room. She shouted back, "You can come with me if you want."

Except for supper, Koby spent the evening alone. The TV in the living room blared nothing but news about Hurricane Lia. In less than twenty-four hours, Lia would come ashore somewhere in the middle Keys. The greatest path of destruction would be ten miles wide.

Koby did not understand why Mom was so set against helping Dad. Was she mad? Did she want him to lose the boats? Or was she just worrying like always? And why hadn't Dad stopped by to check on them? Koby fell asleep puzzling.

She slept hard. When she awoke, dawn had grayed the horizon. Instead of the usual stillness, the rising wind swirled leaves and rattled screen doors. Koby slipped from bed and dressed. She took special care with her leggy. After pulling on her raincoat, she ripped a scrap of paper from her school notebook and scribbled,

> *Mom*
> *I went to help Dad.*
> *Koby*

She left the note on her pillow. Carefully she eased the window open and crawled out through the thick shrubs. Scudding black clouds crowded the blustery sky. Koby untied *Titmouse* and paddled down the canal before starting the engine.

The water was rough, and by the time Koby reached Pelican Harbor, salt water soaked her jeans and sweatshirt. Out at anchor, *Lazy Mae* rocked alongside *Dream Chaser*. Onshore Nickeljack worked, loading a skiff on a trailer. Koby waved to him.

The harbor bristled with activity as Koby pulled alongside *Dream Chaser*. Dutch poked his head topside as she climbed aboard.

"Where's your mother?" he asked with surprise.

"At Tess's."

"Does she know you're here?"

Koby shook her head. "She was still sleeping. I left a note."

Dutch whistled low. "We're going to have Hurricane Paige, too."

"Dad, I want to help."

Dutch regarded her doubtfully. "It will be rough out there."

"I don't care."

"You're bulletproof, mate, I swear. Okay, it's light already. We need to get going. The hurricane is angling a bit north," he said, "so we'll head south. I'm leaving *Dream Chaser* here and taking *Lazy Mae*. Hopefully we can make Banjo Cut on Miner's Key or thereabouts. I figure we have till noon to hole up." Handing Koby several life jackets, he asked, "By the way, have you been aboard lately?"

"No, not since the other day. Why?"

"Someone left a box."

Koby tried to sound casual. "A box? What kind of box?"

"Oh, nothing. Just someone playing a joke."

Koby turned to hide her disappointment.

Dutch kept loading. Armful after armful, he carried tools, charts, and gear onto *Lazy Mae*.

"Can't we leave some of this stuff on *Dream Chaser*?" Koby asked, helping him.

"If the blow comes ashore here—and it looks like it might— there won't be enough left of *Dream Chaser* to hook an anchor to."

"Can't we tow *Dream Chaser* along?"

"Not without a crew."

As Koby carried a load of books aboard *Lazy Mae*, she heard the marine radio crackle, "*Dream Chaser, Dream Chaser*, do you read?"

Koby recognized her mom's voice. She ran to the radio as Dutch walked up behind. He motioned with his hand. "Go ahead and answer; you're the reason she's calling."

Hesitantly Koby picked up the handset. "Yeah, Mom, this is *Dream Chaser*, go ahead."

Paige's guarded voice crackled, "*Dream Chaser*, I'm in the harbor. Do you need more crew?"

TWENTY-EIGHT

"We'll come get you, Mom!" Koby exclaimed.

"Thanks."

"*Dream Chaser* clear," Koby stammered. "Let's go, Dad. Mom's at the dock!"

Dutch rubbed his beard. "You go get her; I'll keep loading."

"No. We'll go together."

"It will save us time if—"

"No!" Koby said. "We'll go together—Mom's waiting."

Dutch grumbled his frustration. "Okay, let's hurry. This blow's breathing down our neck."

They jumped into the large dinghy. Dutch revved the engine and sped toward shore. He paid no attention to his wake. As he reached the dock, he swerved to a stop faster than Koby thought he needed to. Paige, holding a small bag, didn't look as if she needed any more scaring.

"Are you taking both boats?" she asked, scrambling aboard.

Dutch shook his head. "The two of you couldn't handle *Dream Chaser* in rough seas."

Koby glanced ashore and saw Nickeljack watching them from near the boathouse. "What if we had help?" she asked.

"We don't have help."

"Nickeljack could help us—he's worked with lots of boats."

Dutch didn't even look up. "We don't need a derelict to help us drown."

"Dad, he—"

"That old drifter couldn't float a balloon."

"Dad, quit it! He's a captain."

"Used to be—about a million bottles of booze ago."

"If we lose *Dream Chaser*, will the insurance cover her?" Paige asked.

Dutch looked away. "Not by half. There'll be no replacing her."

"Then why not try to save both boats?"

"Yeah, why not ask Nickeljack to help," Koby insisted. "What can you lose—unless you're too proud."

"You're getting a real smart mouth, mate," Dutch said. "Nobody in their right mind would hire that bum."

Angry, Koby scrambled onto the dock. "He's not a bum. You and everybody else just treat him like one! I told Mom you wanted help, but you don't!" She ran up the dock toward Nickeljack, who stood watching.

"Wait a second!" Dutch shouted.

Koby kept running. Her tears made everything blur.

"Looks like we won't be needing rain with all them tears," Nickeljack said as she approached.

Koby didn't know what to do. She sat down on the grass and buried her face against her knees. Nickeljack didn't speak, but Koby didn't mind. She liked having him near. For all his snarling and gruffness, she knew he cared.

Koby heard the hollow sound of footsteps on the wooden dock. She looked up to see Paige carrying her bag toward shore. Dutch sat in the dinghy, shaking his head.

"Let's go back to Tess's," Paige said, walking up. Her voice cracked. "You're right—your father doesn't want help."

Reluctantly Koby stood. She looked at Nickeljack. His deep hooded eyes gave no clue of what he was thinking. He smiled sadly and nodded good-bye.

Dutch yelled something, and Koby looked up to see her dad coming toward them.

"Wait!" he shouted.

Paige tugged on Koby's arm, but Koby drew back.

Dutch jogged up, breathing hard. "Don't leave."

"Why not?" Paige said.

Dutch caught his breath. "Because I'm a bullheaded jackass." He turned to Nickeljack. "I need to get *Dream Chaser* down to Miner's Key. Could you help us?"

Nickeljack's face turned blank with surprise.

"I'm asking you to captain her," Dutch said quietly.

Nickeljack rubbed his chin. "I ain't much of a sailor."

"We'd motor down," Dutch said.

"I don't know, it's been years. Most people wouldn't trust me now with a bobber."

Koby stepped forward and motioned to Nickeljack as if she had a secret.

He stooped with a puzzled look.

Cupping her hand to his ear, Koby whispered, "Please say yes or no—don't make him beg."

The old man straightened slowly and stared out toward *Dream Chaser*. His leathery cheeks twitched. Finally he turned to Dutch and nodded. "Okay, let's get moving."

Dutch mopped a sleeve across his brow. "Thanks. If we can, let's try to make Banjo Cut on Miner's Key. Nickeljack, what do you need to take along?"

"Just Squid."

"Squid?" Dutch looked puzzled. "We'll have plenty to eat."

"You don't want to eat Squid." Nickeljack winked at Koby, who giggled.

"I like squid," Dutch said.

Koby whistled, and the fat basset hound crawled out from behind a stack of lobster pots. He ambled toward them. "Dad, that's Squid," Koby said.

"We might need an extra barge to haul him," Nickeljack said.

Koby crouched and greeted the panting hound. "I'll take care of him."

"Okay," Dutch said. "Let's move. I'll go it alone on *Lazy Mae*. She'll ride rough. The rest of you crew *Dream Chaser*." He turned to Paige. "Are you still crew?"

Paige hesitated. "Wouldn't it be safer for Koby on land?"

"Not if we can dodge the hurricane."

Paige put an arm around Koby's shoulders. "Okay, then, let's get busy!"

By the time *Lazy Mae* and *Dream Chaser* pulled anchor, the harbor bristled with activity. Those boat owners who had decided to stay worked at tying off extra lines. Others were on the move, their skippers gambling they could outrun the storm. The sky had a dull metal look, the air an ominous and restless feel.

As the two boats cleared the harbor onto open water, *Lazy Mae* led the way, plowing through the chop. Aboard *Dream Chaser*, Nickeljack steadied the helm as if he'd been born with it in his hand. His gaze swept the horizon like a radar scope. He reached and adjusted the throttle. "Seas are building fast," he said.

"Will we be okay?" Koby asked.

Nickeljack shrugged. "Might be . . . if we make it to Miner's Key."

"*Dream Chaser, Dream Chaser*, this is the *Lazy Mae*. Do you read?" crackled the radio.

Nickeljack picked up the handset. "Go ahead, *Lazy Mae*."

"Hurricane Center says Lia is headed straight for Lonesome Key."

TWENTY-NINE

Lazy Mae growled at the ocean, bucking along, her red hull smashing whitecaps and sending plumes of spray high over her wheelhouse. Close behind, *Dream Chaser* rode the swells like a lazy giant, lifting and settling, knifing the waves. Her motor hummed. The dinghies bobbed along in tow, carefree.

All boats were different, Koby thought. Kind of like people.

Dutch's voice broke over the radio. "How's it going?"

Nickeljack kept his gaze on the water as he picked up the handset. "Be happier when we reach Banjo Cut."

"Call me if things get too bad."

"*Dream Chaser* will handle it better than your tub," Nickeljack said.

"I'm afraid you're right."

They signed off and continued without speaking. *Dream Chaser*'s masts moaned as stinging spray whipped off the whitecaps. Occasionally the hull shuddered. During the lulls, the radio crackled with static and urgent talk between other boats.

"The wind's getting grabby," Nickeljack said during a lull.

Paige nodded, gripping the rail so tightly that her knuckles showed white.

"Are you getting sick?" Koby asked.

Paige shook her head. She stared over her shoulder at the foreboding sky.

Koby laughed. "We're not going to die!"

"You don't know that," Paige said, facing into the wind with stubborn cheeks.

"Quit worrying!" Koby grumped.

It had been an hour since they passed under Three-Mile Bridge from gulfside out onto the open ocean. Koby watched her dad on the *Lazy Mae*. He stood braced behind the wheel, his squatty lobster boat jarring into each wave. Sheets of spray exploded from the bow.

"These kinds of seas break bones," Nickeljack said. He squinted into the wind with defiance. The deep wrinkles etched into his chiseled face looked like battle scars.

The seas grew rougher. Koby headed below to check on Squid. Paige followed after her to get out the life preservers.

For another bruising hour they motored west by southwest. Even *Dream Chaser* started dropping off the mounting swells and slamming into the troughs. The wind began to wail.

Koby and Paige returned topside. "How much farther?" Koby shouted.

Nickeljack pointed to a thin strip of land over the starboard bow. "That's Miner's Key."

Koby ducked her face to the wind. "How come the wind's blowing at us if the hurricane's behind us?"

"'Cause it blows in circles." Nickeljack glanced toward *Lazy Mae*. "That tub ain't made for this—she's taking a beating."

Koby watched with concern. *Lazy Mae* buried her bow each time she plunged between swells. Dutch braced his feet wide, one hand on the wheel, one gripping the side. Even as they watched, a wave knocked him to his knees. He struggled to stand.

"Is he okay?" Paige screamed.

"If he makes it to Banjo Cut!"

For another half hour they glued their eyes on the *Lazy Mae*, watching Dutch fight to keep her afloat. It seemed the pounding would never end. Finally the struggling lobster boat neared shore and gained some shelter. Still bracing himself, Dutch turned and motioned to a narrow break in the mangroves.

Entering the cut, both boats eased their jarring. Thick stands of mangroves shielded the water and brought an eerie calm. The moaning of the wind died.

"Are we safe now?" Paige asked.

"*Only* for now," Nickeljack said.

Half a mile into Banjo Cut, they found a small natural bay. Dutch radioed, "*Dream Chaser*, how's everybody doing?"

"We're floatin', how are you?"

"Beat up. Listen, let's take our chances here. Set anchor so you can swing about. I'll be right over."

"Roger." Nickeljack hung up the handset. He turned to Koby and Paige with a tired grin. "Now comes the real show."

"I'll drop anchor," Koby said, heading for the bow.

Paige started down the companionway. "I'll make sure every-thing below is secure."

Nickeljack waited until Koby lowered the anchor, then he reversed the engine and backed up. The heavy chain fed out with a loud clatter. "Okay," he shouted, "that's far enough. Tie off!"

Koby fastened the chain.

On *Lazy Mae* Dutch had also set anchor. He jumped in the dinghy and ran spring lines from both boats to the mangrove roots.

Sheets of light rain had started falling by the time Dutch returned to *Dream Chaser*. The wind dipped lower into the cut, plucking at the mangroves and roughing the water. Dutch ran his fingers through his beard as he checked the deck one last time. "That's all we can do," he said. "Let's get below."

Nickeljack shook his head. "If it's all the same, I'll sit out the blow aboard *Lazy Mae*. Someone should tend her bilge and anchor."

"Not alone."

"I won't be alone. I'll have Squid. We came here to save two boats. Let's do it."

Dutch bit at his lip. "You're right, she could use somebody aboard, but I'll go. You stay here where it's more comfortable."

Nickeljack snorted, "I didn't come here for a vacation. You got a family to watch, so watch 'em. Koby, can you get that lazy hound of mine?"

Koby waited for Dutch's nod, then ran below. Grunting, she helped the basset hound up the companionway.

"He never was much good at climbing," Nickeljack said, winking at Koby. He wrestled Squid into the dinghy. "You all enjoy the afternoon," he called back.

Above the wind, Koby shouted, "Nickeljack, take care of yourself!" Even louder she yelled, "'*Cause nobody else will!*"

"Call me when you're settled in," Dutch hollered.

Nickeljack nodded. Wind grabbed at his rain slicker as he started the engine and cast off. Before he reached *Lazy Mae*, the howling air swallowed the sound of his outboard.

"Okay, let's get below," Dutch said. He followed Koby down the companionway and latched the doors tightly. He looked around the main salon and nodded his approval.

Paige had stayed busy. Blankets, a first aid kit, and two flashlights were stacked under the table. She had stowed everything else except some food and the life jackets. "Now what do we do?" she asked.

The wind gusted and whipped, howling madly. Sheets of rain pelted *Dream Chaser*'s deck like gravel. Dutch checked the cabin radio, then turned and sat down. "This is the easy part. All we do is wait—the hurricane does the rest."

Paige busied herself cleaning and tidying up. "Looks like a hurricane already hit this place," she said matter-of-factly.

"Only you would notice," Dutch grumbled.

"You're never around to notice."

"At least I don't abandon ship."

"Quit it!" Koby shouted. "Quit fighting! Both of you."

"Mind your own business," Dutch said.

Hurt and angry, Koby looked out the portal. The deck railing kept disappearing into the shrouded gray fury. "This is my business," she said. "Why do you try to be so mean to each other?"

Paige kept wiping the counters. "I don't think we *try* to be mean."

"It comes natural," Dutch said.

Koby glared at her dad.

Paige walked over to the table. "Honey, your father and I just don't always agree." She looked at Dutch. "By the way, thanks, but no thanks, for the chocolates."

"You're the one who sent chocolates."

"I never sent you anything."

"Someone did."

"Well, don't look at me."

"Then who . . ."

Awkward silence filled the cabin as two pairs of eyes settled on Koby.

"You wouldn't know anything about this, would you?" Paige said.

Koby looked down, fingering the edge of the table.

"Why would you pull a stunt like that?" Dutch asked.

"You two won't say you're sorry, so I thought . . ."

"So you thought you would do it for us, huh?"

"To make you stop fighting. You guys always fight." Koby burst into tears. "If I hadn't lost my dumb foot, maybe you guys wouldn't fight so much."

"No, honey," Paige said, coming over and putting her arm around Koby's shoulders. "The accident was our fault. We're the ones who let you go out riding."

Dutch raised his voice. "That accident was *no one's* fault! Sure, maybe Koby should've been more careful, but kids are kids. If you found one that was careful all the time, you'd have a sideshow freak." Dutch stood and paraded around the salon like a ringmaster at a circus. "Step right up, ladies and gentlemen. We have the one, the only, the girl who was always careful!"

"Quit it," Paige said. "Koby would have both feet if she had been more careful."

Dutch slapped the table. "Everybody rides bikes when they're eight. You can't lock a kid in a padded cell to rot. That's not what growing up is about."

"A missing foot sure isn't what growing up is about," Paige said.

Dutch shook his head, his voice softer. "Maybe it is. Tell me who else's kid would stand out on the sand flats all night to save two whales."

As Paige was about to answer, the radio crackled. "*Dream Chaser, Dream Chaser*, this is *Lazy Mae*."

Dutch crossed quickly to the radio and picked up the handset. "Go ahead, *Lazy Mae*."

"Old Squid and I are tucked in tight. Is everything cozy over there?"

"It could be cozier," Dutch said, eyeing Paige and Koby.

"Mind if I raid the refrigerator here?"

"Make yourself at home."

"Heard anything more on the hurricane?"

"Just what I'm hearing outside," Dutch said.

"We must be tuned to the same program. Good luck."

"Same to you—stay in touch. This is *Dream Chaser*, clear."
Dutch turned from the radio. "Well, folks, sit back, relax, and
enjoy this fine event—brought to you compliments of the
Florida Keys Tourism Bureau. Anyone bring popcorn?"

Neither Koby nor Paige spoke. Dutch lowered himself back
beside the table. As he did, a sharp gust rocked *Dream Chaser*.
Koby stiffened and waited. When a second blast failed to hit,
Paige breathed deeply. "You're right, the accident was no one's
fault. But it happened, and now Koby's whole life—"

"That car wrecked her foot. It didn't wreck her life! Not
unless we let it."

"Dad's right," Koby said.

Paige bit at her lip. "If you had your way, Dutch, she would
live as crazy as you!"

"Beats living in a padded cell."

Koby covered her ears and screamed, "Stop it! Stop fighting
over me. Can't you stop fighting and let me live my own life?"

An awkward silence made the wind and the pelting rain seem
louder. The boat rocked with great rolling motions, but nobody
seemed to notice.

"It's not you we're fighting about," Paige said. "This has to do
with your father being gone all the time."

"I don't see anybody else in this family helping make ends
meet," Dutch said. "The harder I work, the more you complain,
Paige."

Paige gripped the edge of the table. "You're the one who said I
shouldn't work if we lived on a boat. But that's all I've done, keeping this thing shipshape, is work. And no one appreciates it."

Outside the storm grew more violent. Inside, as they shouted to be heard over the shrieking wind, something much stronger than water and wind buffeted them.

"You never do anything but complain," Dutch said. "Have you ever thought of offering even a thimbleful of encouragement?"

"Mom, it's no fun to come home when you get mad all the time."

"And you think I get mad for the fun of it?"

"That had occurred to me," Dutch said.

Koby glared at her dad. "No, Mom," she said. "But why worry so much?"

"Because you two fools chase around the ocean like maniacs."

"We chase around like thousands of other people who live on the ocean," Dutch said. "That doesn't mean you have to worry all the time. Koby has to learn to take care of herself. We won't be there her whole life."

"Mom," Koby said. "Other moms love their kids, but they don't worry like you."

"Koby's right," Dutch said.

Paige turned defiantly. "Dutch, if it hadn't been for me, Koby would still be out holding whales on the sand flats. You sure weren't about to go out looking. Don't you see! She already lost a foot. What if she had drowned?"

"And what if she had?" Dutch said. "What if a meteorite hit? What if the world ended? Just because of one accident, we can't live our lives afraid of another."

"Stop it!" Koby screamed again. "I feel like a scrap of fish being fought over by two stubborn pelicans. Don't I have any say?"

Paige started sobbing as *Dream Chaser* lurched hard to port.

"We better get ready for the worst of this blow," Dutch said. Even as he spoke, *Dream Chaser* swung around hard and heeled sharply. Dutch grabbed the life jackets. "Here, put these on."

Dream Chaser lifted sideways as if a big hand had shoved her. She pivoted back and forth wildly.

"I hope the anchor and spring lines hold," Dutch shouted. He grabbed the handset. "*Lazy Mae, Lazy Mae*, how you doing?"

At first there was no reply. Then Nickeljack's garbled and distorted voice came on. "I'll tell you in an hour. I'm busy now."

"Good luck!" Dutch shouted. He hung up the handset.

Rain whipped sideways past the portholes. The wind keened. Suddenly something jarred *Dream Chaser*, sending a shudder through the hull.

"What was that?" Paige screamed.

"Either we're drifting loose or the keel bottomed. This bay is shallow."

A stronger jar sent Koby sprawling to the floor. One of the cupboards popped open. Boxes and cans spilled out and ricocheted about, hitting Koby. Paige frantically helped her back to her seat. The wind had become a shrieking wall of sound, prying, grabbing, shoving. A loud crack echoed through the hull, then something struck the deck with a metallic crash.

"I think we've lost a mast!" Dutch yelled.

Koby braced herself any way she could. The next sharp tilt

sent Paige slipping under the table. Koby grabbed for her, but it was Dutch who reached down and pulled her up. Bracing his feet, he held her tightly. Paige wrapped her arms around Dutch.

The hurricane became a nightmare of evil sounds and violent movements. Like a bucking bull, *Dream Chaser* heaved and twisted. Koby feared the hull would crack open like an egg. At one point she closed her eyes to try and make it all go away.

For a maddening eternity the storm's berserk fury came unleashed. When it seemed it would never end, the wailing wind finally dulled to a moan. The rain slanted downward instead of across the portals. Bit by bit, *Dream Chaser*'s wild rocking eased.

When no vicious gusts had struck for several minutes, Dutch reached and picked up the handset. "*Lazy Mae, Lazy Mae*, this is *Dream Chaser*, do you read me?" No answer. Again he keyed the handset. "*Lazy Mae, Lazy Mae*, this is *Dream Chaser*, are you there?" Tension strained his voice. Still no answer.

Dutch worked his way to a portal and tried to look out. "Can't see a thing," he said. He slammed his fist on the table. "I should have been the one to stay aboard *Lazy Mae*. She's not as seaworthy as *Dream Chaser*."

THIRTY

Dutch prowled restlessly, pausing now and then to squint out the portals at the swirling sheets of rain. Twice more he tried to raise *Lazy Mae* on the radio. Still, no answer.

"I was a fool," he muttered.

"For what?" Paige asked. "Trying to save the boats?"

"For trying to save the *Lazy Mae*. That boat's not made for this kind of blow."

"Do you think Nickeljack is all right?" Koby asked.

"Hard to say. It wouldn't take much to swamp *Lazy Mae*'s open hull. One good thing—here in Banjo Cut you can't sink far. I doubt it's ten feet deep." Dutch kept peering out.

"We should have left the boats in Pelican Harbor," Paige said.

"You would have liked seeing them both go down."

"No, I would not have liked it," Paige said. "I know how much they mean to you. But are two boats worth risking some-one's life?"

"Paige, they're all I have now! And in this kind of blow, nobody's safe anywhere!"

Koby watched her mom turn away without speaking—she

looked to be fighting back tears. For the next hour the three of them waited. Koby hated the grim silence.

Dutch kept pacing and looking. Suddenly he grabbed his slicker. "I'm going topside; I think I see something."

"What?" Paige asked.

"Don't know. Something's out there."

"Be careful."

Dutch touched his finger to Paige's chin in an awkward, gentle way. "You're worrying again."

"I wasn't worrying, just telling you to be careful."

When Dutch opened the companionway, the wind shrieked and snatched at his slicker. Rain drove down into the salon. Quickly he stepped out and pulled the doors closed. Again the storm sounded muffled. Koby looked at her mom. Paige had said she wasn't worrying, but she was biting at her lip and staring out the portal with a haunted gaze. Koby twisted at a loose thread on her own life preserver.

The doors opened again and Dutch backed quickly down the steps. He had to fight the wind to close the doors from inside.

"See anything?" Paige asked.

Dutch nodded. "The *Lazy Mae* sank—she's down in shallow water. Her wheelhouse is still clear, and the dinghy is afloat. Nickeljack and Squid are on top, lying flat as starfish."

"Is Nickeljack okay?" Koby asked.

"I waved to him, and he waved back."

"Does he have a life jacket on?"

Dutch smiled. "Yup, and so does Squid. Silliest thing I ever saw."

"How can we help him?" Paige asked.

"We can't, yet. We'll get dry clothes ready and something hot for him to drink. When the wind lets up, he'll bring the dinghy over."

As Paige heated water, Koby rummaged through her dad's closet to find dry clothes. Everything was too big for the skinny old captain. Finally she picked out a pair of wool pants, a sweatshirt, thick socks, and a belt.

Back in the salon, Dutch sat brooding, drumming his fingernails on the table.

"Will these be okay?" Koby asked, setting the folded clothes beside him.

"Yeah," Dutch grunted, not bothering to look up.

Koby sat down quietly. The boat rocked less and less.

Dutch rubbed his eyes. "I should have known when to quit," he said. "But I wanted so badly to live on the ocean. I wanted to make my living here."

"What's wrong with that?" Koby asked.

"Nothing, unless you ignore when the ocean says no."

"What else would you do?"

"Onshore, plenty. I've built houses for years. After this storm there will be plenty of work."

"Could we still live on *Dream Chaser*?" Koby ventured.

Dutch glanced at Paige. "Depends."

Paige looked up from where she was heating water in the galley. Before she could speak, a muffled whine sounded above the wind.

"The dinghy!" Koby shouted.

Dutch leaped up and bounded for the companionway. Koby followed on his heels. This time the wind did not grab at the doors. Topside, they spotted Nickeljack working the dinghy through rough water toward the stern. In the front sat Squid, still wearing his life jacket. The fat basset hound always looked sad. Now he looked seasick.

Nickeljack threw Dutch the bowline and killed the engine.

"Glad to see you!" Dutch shouted.

The old captain looked gaunt and pale, dripping water like a drowned rat. He nodded and reached for Squid. Dutch bent down and helped hoist the hound onto the deck.

Nickeljack clambered aboard. "Not much of a way to spend an afternoon," he grumped. "I'm sorry about the *Lazy Mae*."

"How did she go down?" Dutch asked.

"Her bilges stayed pumped till a wave put us on our side. I heard the hull crack. Lucky for Squid, *Lazy Mae* righted going down. Almost had to give that hound swimming lessons. Dumb dog hates water."

"*I* was the fool for bringing the *Lazy Mae* out here," Dutch said. "You did everything you could!"

Paige handed Nickeljack the dry clothes. "Here, get into these." She ushered him below deck and forward into the V-berth.

"Koby," Dutch said. "Let's check the damage. We'll spend the night here and head back in the morning."

"I'll get us something to eat," Paige called up.

Topside, Dutch and Koby looked around. Dutch had been

right. The rear mast rested bent across the foredeck. There was other damage, but not a lot. *Titmouse* needed bailing.

"Before heading home, we'll dive and check the keel," Dutch said, working his way around the deck. He stopped and gazed out at the choppy waves that surrounded *Lazy Mae*'s wheelhouse. Slowly he lowered his chin in reverence as if standing over a grave. "You were a good lady, *Lazy Mae*," he said, his voice soft. "You'll get more lobster on you this way than with me aboard." For a moment the wind paused, and Dutch looked around at Koby with a smile. "I still have me a one-legged pirate—I'd say I'm plenty lucky." He motioned. "C'mon, let's go get some chow."

Koby followed her dad below. Nickeljack had changed and was drinking hot coffee, regaining his grizzled composure sip by sip. Dutch's clothes draped loosely on his bony frame. Squid still looked seasick.

Koby knelt down to pet the hound. "Let's get you something to eat."

"Don't treat him too nice," Nickeljack said, "or he'll want to come back out for another storm."

"I doubt that." Koby hugged the sad-looking hound.

While Paige fixed food, Dutch worked the radio to get news of the hurricane. Reception was bad, but he finally raised someone. From the sound of it, Hurricane Lia had passed between Lonesome Key and Donner's Key to the north. Both islands had taken a bad beating.

"We guessed right," Dutch said. "I'd hate to have been up in Colter's Cut during the blow."

Nickeljack ran a finger in circles on the table. "There's gonna be a lot of sad stories."

That evening brought more rain. Dutch checked the anchor before nightfall. Paige prepared the V-berth for Nickeljack and Squid. Koby made her bed on one of the couches in the salon and stretched out. For the first time since the hurricane, she thought about Lady and Squirt. Could they have lived through this terrible storm? Had Max let them go? Koby curled her knees to her chest and pulled the pillow fearfully under her head.

"Well, good night, Koby. We'll see you in the morning," Dutch said, closing up the companionway.

Paige came from the stateroom, a pillow and blanket under her arm. "I'll sleep out here with Koby."

"Whatever you like," Dutch said.

"It's what I'd like."

Koby rolled over to hide her tears.

The next morning, everybody rose by daybreak. Koby and Dutch took out masks and dived on *Dream Chaser*'s keel. They could find no damage. Koby noticed how thick the barnacles were on the hull and remembered Nickeljack saying, "You don't chase dreams with barnacles on your hull from not putting out!"

Koby bailed the water from T*itmouse*, then she and Dutch took both dinghies over and dived on the *Lazy Mae*. Reluctantly they admitted there was little worth saving.

"Insurance will be all we get off her," Dutch said, coming up for the last time.

By midmorning, they pulled anchor and motored out of Banjo Cut. A light chop stirred the gray and turbid water. Heavy clouds hung low.

Paige remained below deck. Koby sat on the bow pulpit, holding Squid across her lap. The hound looked especially sad-eyed. Dutch stood at the helm, a faraway look in his eyes. Nickeljack crouched aft, staring at the water and at the dinghies that bobbed lightly on the rolling stern wave. Everybody seemed lost in their own world.

Not until they crossed under Three-Mile Bridge to gulfside did they gather around the helm. With binoculars they inspected the hurricane's damage. Each person noticed something different. Koby looked for a small gray house she often used as a bearing marker. It had completely disappeared. Paige motioned ashore to where several boats lay upside down on people's lawns.

"Look there," Dutch said, pointing. A long row of buildings upshore had collapsed as if stomped on by a huge foot.

"I hope Lady and Squirt are okay," Koby said, as they passed the canal leading to Max's boat basin.

Nickeljack shook his head, a sad faraway gaze in his eyes. "Why? So they can live the rest of their lives in a big swimming pool?"

"Tracy said they would let them go," Koby said.

Nickeljack spoke sharply. "Quit kidding yourself!"

The damage increased as they motored northward. From the

distance, docks, fences, and trees looked like strewn garbage. When *Dream Chaser* rounded the channel markers into Pelican Harbor, a churchlike silence fell over the deck. The harbor looked as if a giant hand had reached down from the clouds and stirred everything. All the boats had been destroyed—except for a couple of dinghies that floated patiently behind their upended or sunken mother ships.

"Lord!" breathed Nickeljack.

A few people milled along the shoreline. When *Dream Chaser* entered the harbor, these people stopped and stared as if seeing a ghost.

Dutch aimed the bow toward a damaged but standing section of dock. "We sure appreciated your help, Nickeljack. We'll make it up to you somehow."

"I wish I could have kept *Lazy Mae* afloat."

"Nothing could have done that," Dutch said.

Nickeljack boosted Squid ashore and scrambled after him. He turned with a sad smile. "Thanks for letting me try."

Dutch reached over the rail and shook the old captain's hand. "You done good—you done *real* good!"

Clothes crumpled but shoulders square, Nickeljack strode up the dock. Twenty feet behind, Squid ambled along at his own pace.

Dutch rested his hands on the helm. "So, what now?"

Paige looked down. "I don't know."

"Somebody decide," Koby said.

THIRTY-ONE

"It looks like this crew needs to throw anchor for a powwow," Dutch said.

Koby and Paige nodded as they all sat down around the cockpit. Koby had a strange feeling—the same feeling as when she added one more breath to a full balloon. If this balloon popped, everything would be over. Forever.

"So," Dutch began. "What are we going to do?"

"Things have to change," Paige said quietly.

"What do you mean?"

"You two being gone all the time. Me stranded on this boat, wondering if I even have a family."

"So, what do you want? You want us to stay here on the boat with you all the time?"

"Not all the time. But a family needs to spend time together."

Dutch nodded reluctantly.

"Dad, I have an idea," Koby said. "We should take *Dream Chaser* out every week."

"That has nothing to do with this," Dutch said, his voice prickling with irritation.

"It does," Koby said. "You want to know what Nickeljack said?"

"What's that?"

"He said that *Dream Chaser* isn't your dream, it's your dumb pride. He said you can't chase dreams with barnacles on your hull from not putting out."

"Nickeljack said that?"

Koby nodded hesitantly. "He said *Dream Chaser* is a mighty fancy bed. Dad, he's right! If we don't go out, we might as well live in a house."

Dutch stood and looked over the stern toward the seawall. He cleared his throat. "Maybe Nickeljack is right." He turned and looked at Paige. "Would you be willing to try living aboard *Dream Chaser* again?"

Paige shook her head. "It's not living on a boat I mind, it's being stranded out here in the middle of the harbor—you two gone all the time. That's no family."

"But we only have two dinghies," Koby said.

"Okay, then, you'll understand if *Titmouse* is mine from now on."

"Uh . . . I think you're absolutely right," Koby said quickly. "Nobody should be stranded out here."

"Whatever happens," Paige said, "I'm going to keep working at the marina office."

"But with insurance and me working, we should have enough money."

"I have my pride, too," Paige said.

Dutch sat down again and nodded. "As soon as I settle the

insurance on *Lazy Mae*, I'll catch up payments on *Dream Chaser* and move her into a slip."

"As soon as they're rebuilt," Paige added.

"Yeah, and if Mom's helping earn money, Dad, you can be home more." As soon as the words slipped out, Koby felt two sets of eyes settle on her. "And I can be home more, too, huh?" she added quickly.

Paige and Dutch nodded.

"So, are we going to give it another try?" Dutch said.

Paige twisted at the sleeve of her T-shirt. She looked away and shook her head. "I'm just not sure it will work."

"It can," Koby said. "If you and Dad just won't fight."

Paige looked up. "You're sure full of advice today, young lady. You won't even come home when you're told."

"I will!" Koby said. "I promise, I promise, I promise."

"Unless she finds more whales of course," Dutch chided.

Koby poked out her tongue.

Paige smiled sadly at Koby. "You are right, though, honey. Arguing is something this boat has too much of."

When nobody spoke, the air became tense. Finally Dutch rubbed his beard and repeated quietly, "So . . . what are we going to do?"

"I'm up for staying aboard!" Koby exclaimed.

"As a family?" Paige asked, her chin quivering.

"As a family," Dutch answered quietly.

Koby threw her arms around both of her parents' necks, and

they all hugged tightly in a circle. This time nobody let go for a long, long while. When they finally did, everybody blinked at wet eyes.

Dutch breathed deeply. "So, what do we do first?"

Koby spoke hesitantly. "Can we go see Lady and Squirt?"

Dutch nodded. "The captain's dinghy will be departing in two minutes."

They laughed.

"I wonder how Tess did during the hurricane." Koby said.

"When I left, she decided to drive north to Orlando to stay with family," Paige said. "She should be all right."

Soon they piled aboard the dinghy and headed in. Dutch pulled up onshore because the dock looked unsafe. Rubble lay scattered everywhere. It was as if a giant garbage truck had backed up to Pelican Harbor and dumped its load. People wandered about, appearing lost.

Together the three of them hiked up from the shore. They stopped in their tracks as they entered the parking lot. Four cars, including their station wagon, lay crushed under a telephone pole. They stared in disbelief. Paige put a hand to her mouth. Dutch whistled low.

After inspecting the station wagon, Koby asked, "Could we take the dinghy over?"

Dutch shook his head. "Too rough out."

"But how can we check on the whales?"

"Maybe life is telling us to walk," Dutch said, allowing a smile. "We haven't been on a good walk in years."

"It's over three miles," Paige said, looking at Koby.

"Three of us have five good legs," Dutch said. "That should be plenty. If it isn't, we'll go piggyback. Haven't done that in a while either, huh, mate?"

Koby still felt argued over. "I weigh a ton, Dad," she said.

"Oh, yeah, a fat one like you probably weighs two tons."

Koby drew her leggy back to kick him.

Dutch jumped aside. "I'm sorry, I didn't mean it. I swear that leggy would dent a tank."

"My secret weapon," Koby kidded.

Holding hands, they crossed the parking lot, Dutch in the middle. Near the road, Nickeljack stood talking to three men. Koby waved, and he waved back.

"I see the hurricane didn't wreck everything!" Nickeljack shouted.

"No, it sure didn't!" Dutch hollered back, squeezing Paige and Koby's hands tightly.

Koby felt as if she were floating. Being on a walk with Mom and Dad seemed like the grandest thing in the world.

A mile down the road, Koby's stump grew sore. Dutch let her jump up for a piggyback ride. The rest of the way to the basin, she held to her dad's broad shoulders like a little kid, not minding.

Arriving, Koby slid down. She looked toward the basin with concern. Although the whales were farther away from the hurricane than Pelican Harbor, she remembered how bad the storm had been even in Banjo Cut.

She held her breath and listened. Faintly, a whale's blow

could be heard. Not waiting for her parents, Koby dashed around the house and raced toward the basin. Max and Tracy were there, standing beside the water.

"How are they? How are they?" Koby shouted.

Tracy turned and gave Koby a big hug as she ran up. "They've been through a storm like the rest of us," she said. "But they made it, and I think they're all right."

Koby looked down into the basin. Lady and Squirt were floating along the side wall. Squirt had a raw scrape on his left side. Koby pointed. "What happened to him?"

"We had a tidal surge. Lady was all right, but it dumped Squirt up on the lawn. In the middle of the hurricane, Max and a volunteer ran out and were able to shove him back in."

"Why didn't you let them go?"

"We didn't have time."

"Will he be okay?" Koby pointed at Squirt.

Tracy nodded. "It's no worse than a skinned knee."

Dutch and Paige came walking up.

"Where were you all during the storm?" Tracy asked.

"Out on *Dream Chaser*," Koby said.

"On the water?"

Koby nodded.

"How did it go?"

Koby told Tracy and Max all about their adventure. She didn't say anything about Mom and Dad getting back together again, except she ended with, "So, now we're *all* living on *Dream Chaser* again."

Tracy studied Paige and Dutch's faces with a faint smile. "Well, that sounds good."

"When can Lady and Squirt be let go?" Koby asked.

"Another couple of weeks and we'll move them out of here."

"You're going to let them go, aren't you?" Koby asked strongly.

"Yes, that's the plan."

THIRTY-TWO

The damage from Hurricane Lia had been bad. North, on Donner's Key, whole blocks of houses were flattened. It was lucky Tess Morgan had driven up to Orlando to stay with family. The tidal surge destroyed many homes along her canal, including hers.

School was canceled for a week because the roof on the Lonesome Key Junior High School had ripped partly off. This gave Koby plenty of time to visit the whales. She also helped Dutch work on *Dream Chaser*. Within two days he had the broken mast fixed.

One afternoon, Koby found him cleaning the hull. She offered to help. Dutch agreed, and together they used scuba gear to scrape barnacles. Even though it was hard, she enjoyed working underwater with her dad.

Word spread around the harbor of what Nickeljack had done trying to save *Lazy Mae*. Koby noticed more people stopping to talk to the old captain. Nickeljack kept being his old snarly self, and Squid kept right on being a lazy hound dog with a who-cares attitude.

Dutch borrowed a friend's car so he could start looking for work. Within a week, he had enough house repair jobs to last a year. Paige worked daily in the office at the marina. Koby noticed a change in her mom. Each evening, Paige talked excitedly about things she had seen or done that day.

Two things still bothered Koby. Although her parents were together again and weren't arguing, there remained a coldness between them. Never did they touch or hold hands. Also, the whales worried Koby. Nickeljack insisted they were going to be sent to an aquarium. Tracy insisted that would never happen.

One day after school, Koby stopped to visit Nickeljack. As she crouched to pet Squid, the old captain said, "I see your parents tightened their knot some."

Koby nodded.

A thin smile warmed Nickeljack's eyes. "Sometimes good knots come loose—then you snug them back up again. But sometimes if knots don't hold, they weren't meant to. Then you got to quit pulling. Understand?"

Koby nodded, not wanting to. As she stood to leave, a man pulled up to the curb and stepped from his Cadillac. His bright red shirt was printed with yellow pineapples and hung over his belly like a curtain. He surveyed the damage with his hands on his hips. "Howdy, folks, I'm from up north," he said, strolling toward them. "I understand you had a hurricane?"

Nickeljack spit on the ground. "Hurricane?" he said. "That little blow weren't hardly a squall. In fact I took my hound out on the water and enjoyed it."

"You mean you took a boat out?" the man asked incredulously.

"Yup," Nickeljack drawled. "We laid right out on top and watched the whole thing. Weren't nothing. Nothing at all." He spit again.

Koby turned away to choke off a giggle. The fat tourist shook his head and returned to his Cadillac.

After the man left, Nickeljack didn't say a word. Not a word. He just winked at Koby.

At the basin, Squirt's scrape healed fast, aided by another batch of Nickeljack's paste. The whale calf nursed every fifteen minutes, day and night. Almost magically, both whales kept improving. Soon their skins glistened black and healthy. Squealing to each other, they tossed their heads like happy puppies whenever Koby arrived. Around and around the basin they raced, black bullets beneath a mirrored surface.

No mention was made of releasing the whales. Whenever Koby asked, Max and Tracy would say, "Soon."

One day Squirt threw Koby a piece of seaweed. She threw it back, and he started playing keep-away. Whenever she swam close, he slapped his tail and rocketed around upside down, his pale belly shimmering. Koby had no choice but to declare him the winner. After that, Squirt learned to bring a piece of seaweed whenever he wanted to play.

Without realizing it, Koby found she was communicating with the whales. A whistle or slap of her hand brought the whales to her side. Sometimes she needed only to motion. They made sounds—squeals, clicks, whistles, groans, buzzes, wheezing, scratchy and popping sounds, squawks, clacks, groaning, shrill cries, and creaking like a rusty hinge. Everything meant something. Koby often tried to mimic the sounds.

Other things happened. Each day they played ball. Lady enjoyed towing Koby with her fin. Sometimes when she did, thin trickles of bubbles streamed from the sides of her mouth as if she were laughing. A couple of times she let out explosive bursts of air. Squirt would follow, leaping higher and higher from the water, twisting in playful excitement and crashing with delight on his side.

Still there was no talk of release.

In the evenings, Koby rested with the whales in the shallows near the boat ramp. She wished these quiet times would never end—lying there, talking, daydreaming, looking into their inquiring eyes. The whales seemed so understanding and wise.

It was during one of these times, as the sun disappeared into the ocean like a sinking shimmering beach ball, that Tracy stopped by. She watched Koby and the whales for a long while before speaking. Koby sensed something awkward in the silence. Finally, Tracy said, "Well, Koby, your friends are ready to go home. Tomorrow we set them free."

THIRTY-THREE

The words "Tomorrow we set them free" stunned Koby. She wanted the whales to swim free again in the ocean—it was what she had dreamed of. It was what everybody had worked hard for. But that day had always been next week or next month. Now Koby felt like crying.

"We plan to let them go late tomorrow afternoon," Tracy said.

"You're really going to let them go?"

Tracy nodded. "A lot of people will be motoring out to watch. If you want to invite someone special, you can."

"Can I bring Mom and Dad and Nickeljack and a friend from school?"

"Maybe not that many."

"Please, just four?"

The tall veterinarian studied Koby, then nodded with a smile. "Okay, we'll make room."

"Thanks." Koby stared at the two whales. She rubbed at her eyes.

Tracy squeezed Koby's shoulder. "Are you all right?"

Koby had that feeling again—being happy and very sad at the same time. She forced a thin smile, blinking. "Yeah, sure. I better go." She turned and ran toward the dinghy. Quickly she climbed into *Titmouse* and headed out.

With hardly a breeze, the little boat skittered across the washboard surface. Koby didn't much enjoy the ride. Once when a good friend of hers had moved to California, Koby had cried. But this was different. She and Shawna still wrote to each other. You couldn't write to a whale.

As Koby entered Pelican Harbor, she saw Dad's dinghy tied off to *Dream Chaser*. "Mom! Dad!" she yelled, pulling alongside.

Dutch poked his head topside. "Hi, mate!"

"Tomorrow they're letting the whales free. Can you and Mom go along and watch?"

"Don't see why not."

"Good, we'll leave after school." She pushed off and waved. "I have to go tell Nickeljack."

She found him out on the dock working on an old wood-hulled trawler. Squid rested nearby, watching the world with only one lazy eye open.

Nickeljack waved as she approached.

Koby called, "They're letting the whales loose."

"I'll believe that when I see it," Nickeljack grumped.

Koby smiled. "Will you come watch tomorrow?"

"Those whales don't need me wrecking their big day."

"Will you come along, for me? Please?"

"Why would you want that?"

"'Cause we're friends."

Nickeljack stood and wiped his hands on a rag. "What would I do with Squid?"

"Bring him along—I'll pick you up after school."

Before Nickeljack could answer, Koby started the engine and angled back toward *Dream Chaser*. She hoped Tracy didn't mind an extra four-legged passenger.

The next day at school, Becky Norman jumped at the chance to go watch the whale release. When the last bell finally rang, she and Koby rode the bus to Pelican Harbor. They wiggled in their seats with anticipation.

Koby found Nickeljack working on the same wood-hulled boat. She hollered to him that she would be back to pick him up in five minutes. The old captain shook his head and grumbled something. Koby ignored him. As she climbed into *Titmouse*, she peeked back and smiled. Nickeljack was putting away his tools.

Dutch and Paige were already waiting aboard *Dream Chaser*. Becky explored the sailboat while Koby changed into a swimsuit.

"Koby," Dutch called. "Why don't you and Becky take Nickeljack in *Titmouse*? Your mother and I will follow with our dinghy."

"Okay," Koby answered. Soon she and Becky had picked up Nickeljack and Squid. Weighted down, they plowed out of Pelican Harbor and south toward the boat basin. Becky kept staring at Nickeljack.

The other dinghy followed, Dutch sitting in the stern, Paige in the bow. The two might as well have been on opposite sides of the Grand Canyon, Koby thought. She almost wished they *would* argue a little. Instead they had taken to speaking politely all the time but never laughing or holding hands. Koby had to admit she didn't feel much like laughing or hugging, either, after all that had happened. She did miss the tricks she and Dad used to play on each other.

When they arrived at the basin, boats lined both sides of the canal. Max had decided to tow the whales out cradled in two huge Navy dinghies. These would be towed by powerboats. Slowly the dinghies were deflated and slid under the whales, then reinflated. This way, Lady and Squirt never had to leave the water. Because of the heat, the workers stacked bags of ice against each whale and placed wet towels over their backs.

With everything ready, two of the powerboats hooked on to the dinghies with long towlines. Koby rode with Tracy, beside Lady. Before boarding, Koby handed her leggy to her mom. She tucked her mask and fin at her feet. Max and another volunteer rode with Squirt. Everyone else boarded the assorted powerboats. Tracy laughed when she spotted Nickeljack struggling to lift Squid aboard.

People stared from shore as the strange parade of boats worked their way down the canal. Aboard, nobody spoke. When they reached open water, Tracy broke the quiet. "So, Koby, how is your bag of problems?"

Koby thought a moment. "Most of it fits in my pocket."

"What doesn't fit?"

Koby shook her head. "My parents."

"Aren't they together again?"

"Yeah, but it's like we're all on different planets. Nobody hugs or holds hands or jokes like we used to."

"Maybe that will take time."

"Maybe," Koby mumbled.

Again they rode in silence. Koby looked forward and saw her parents standing apart from each other on one of the towboats.

"Tracy," Koby said suddenly. "I'm happy, but I'm sad. Does that make sense?"

Tracy nodded. "All the sense in the world. It's hard to let go of something you love."

"Whales are hard enough, but parents are even harder."

Tracy reached and gave Koby's arm a squeeze. "You're becoming a very wise person, Ms. Koby Easton."

"Will I ever see the whales again?" Koby asked.

"I don't know."

"I won't see you again," Koby said.

"Of course you will—you're a Pod Squad member. Every time there's a stranding, you'll be called. We're like a big family that meets whenever we're needed."

"Do you promise to call me?"

"I promise."

Slowly the boats worked their way out from shore. Tracy wanted to be at least fifteen miles beyond the reef for the release—there the whales would be in water two thousand feet deep. When Koby looked back, the shoreline had disappeared. The cluster of boats rose and fell over gentle rolling swells.

Koby tried to keep busy splashing water on Lady's back. Lady lay completely still as if sensing what was happening. Her big trusting eyes looked about curiously. A lump grew in Koby's throat.

After nearly two hours, Tracy finally raised her hand, signaling the towboats to stop. She looked over at Koby, understanding in her hazel eyes.

"It's time," she said.

THIRTY-FOUR

The two Navy dinghies were drawn close to each other. Engines on the powerboats stopped, and eerie silence settled over the water. Out here in the middle of forever, people's voices sounded distant and small.

"We'll want to free them both at the same moment," Max said.

Carefully they removed the wet towels from the whales' backs and opened air valves to deflate the dinghies. The powerboats grouped nearby, everyone watching intently. All at once someone yelled, "Look, it's a pod of dolphins!"

Koby turned. Sure enough—from this distance she could see dozens and dozens of sharp fins, fast tails, and curving forms slicing and rolling across the distant swells.

"Tracy, if pilot whales are really dolphins, will Lady and Squirt join that pod?" Koby asked.

"There's a good chance they might. Let's release them and see."

As the dinghies lost air and settled deeper, Koby rolled into the water. Lady's eyes glistened.

"Okay," Max called, "let's ease them in."

Koby helped work Lady over the edge. When the big whale was free in the water, Koby adjusted her mask and ducked beneath the surface to watch. The crystal clear water showed sunlight forming long rays that speared deep into the black. Lady hung suspended as if in some great underwater heaven. With a lazy but powerful stroke of her tail, she glided forward.

Koby surfaced. "Hurry up with Squirt!" she yelled.

Aboard the other dinghy, the calf was thrashing violently, as if he knew he was being left behind. The air had been slower escaping that dinghy, and Max could not get him out.

"Hurry!" Tracy shouted. "Get him in the water!"

Still Max and the helper struggled. Finally they dumped Squirt roughly over the edge. Lady had swum some distance away now, moving faster and faster. Squirt floated motionless, as if dazed. When he did skull forward, it was away from his mother.

Everybody aboard the boats and in the water screamed and shouted at the calf, pointing. Squirt moved erratically, searching.

Koby swam after him. "No! No, Squirt!"

And then Lady's sharp and familiar whistle sounded over the waves. Squirt spun in the water. Koby dived in time to see a streak of black slice past her like charred lightning. She surfaced and saw Lady and Squirt join beyond the boats. They came together, spinning, rolling, and flopping—dancing as only whales can dance.

A chorus of cheers and clapping erupted. When the noise died away, Max shouted, "Okay, everybody aboard!"

Those in the water swam as a group toward the powerboats. All except Koby. When she saw Lady and Squirt circling each other, she swam toward them with long even strokes. She had nearly reached them before anyone noticed.

"Koby!" Tracy shouted. "Come back."

Others shouted, too, but Koby ignored them. She had to say good-bye. As she swam closer, Lady suddenly submerged. The next thing Koby felt was the buzzing tickle on her stump from Lady's echolocation. The tingle thrilled her. In her memory and her dreams she would never forget that magical, wonderful sensation.

When Lady surfaced, Koby reached and ran her hand along the whale's head, working her way back until she held to her fin. "Where will you guys go?" she asked.

Only the lapping of water and the call of a seagull answered her. Koby pressed close. For a short while Lady did not move, then she started slowly forward. Koby held to her fin and was towed through the waves. After a short distance, Lady slipped gently beneath the surface and the ride ended—she had said her good-bye. Deliberately she started toward the pod of dolphins now moving abreast of the boats a quarter mile out.

"Good-bye," Koby choked.

The water swirled as Squirt nudged Koby in the rump. Koby turned with a laugh and dove. The screaming from the boats ceased abruptly. Squirt circled in. Koby kicked harder and harder.

Together they spiraled downward. When finally Squirt glided too deep, Koby surfaced for breath. She ignored all the shouting.

Then a deep gruff voice sounded apart from the rest. It was Nickeljack. He was not commanding or pleading, simply stating fact. "Koby, it's time for them to go free!"

Koby turned. "But I love them!" she cried.

"I know you do," Nickeljack called. "That's why you *have* to let them go now."

In that moment, Koby knew that Nickeljack was right. Turning, she swam toward the boat. Squirt streaked past several times, but Koby kept swimming. For a moment the calf disappeared as if he had left. Then with a flash, he returned and flippered a sloppy strand of seaweed in Koby's path. She grabbed the seaweed and kept swimming with it. Squirt darted past, tossing his head, wanting her to throw it back. Koby refused.

As she reached the boat, the calf tagged her in the rump one last time. Koby burst into tears. Without looking back, she hopped up the ladder. Behind her she could hear the calf's loud chattering.

Tracy met her and held her shoulders firmly. "Wait until he leaves before you turn around," she said. "He needs to go to his mother now."

Koby hugged Tracy. "But I'll never see him again. Never! Ever!" She sobbed as she heard Squirt's tail slap the surface of the water.

Her friend held her gently. "Yes, you will. All living things share life. Every time you see dolphins or whales, you'll feel joy in their freedom. You'll share their spirit."

Koby hugged even harder, holding the piece of seaweed tightly in her fist.

"Okay, now you can turn," Tracy said.

Koby turned and saw Squirt heading toward Lady out in the swells. The big, gentle mother was waiting patiently. When they joined, the mother and calf began their ambling journey—a journey that would take them a lifetime. In silence all eyes watched as the two rolling fins grew more distant. Finally they blended into the far-off pod, drifting along, ruffling the surface like a gentle traveling breeze.

"I never dreamed I'd see this day," Max said softly.

Nickeljack spoke—to no one in particular. "This is a good day, I reckon."

"For whales and for people," Tracy said.

Koby turned around and could not find a dry eye. And under all the tears were a lot of smiles. She saw Becky, her eyes red, her cheeks streaked. And she saw Max and Tracy. They smiled tearfully. Even Nickeljack wiped at his leathery cheek with the back of his hand.

Dutch and Paige came over and hugged Koby, one on each side. She stood in the center, balancing without her leggy. As they watched the pod shimmer out of sight, Koby slid the fistful of seaweed into her dad's pocket.

Ben Mikaelsen lives in Bozeman, Montana, with his wife, Melanie, and a six-hundred-pound bear named Buffy. Mr. Mikaelsen's first book for young readers, *Rescue Josh McGuire*, was published by Hyperion in 1991 and won both the Western Writers of America Spur Award and the International Reading Association's Best First Work in the older readers' category.